She had taken a year abroad. Would she survive a season in Hell?

CONNIE SAWYER: Her natural curiosity led her to enroll in a foreign year abroad program. Had it also led her into a death trap in London's student underground?

DELIA SAWYER: All her life she had meekly let her husband make the decisions in her life. Now she had suddenly left him—to rescue her daughter from a mysterious danger . . .

STANLEY THATCHPOLE: The gruff-speaking Midlands industrialist had driven his Rolls-Royce down to London to search for his daughter. He and Delia would now become a team, of sorts . . .

HENRY DANIELS: The missing student had simply been home with the flu, or so his mother insisted. But was it a macabre coincidence that a few days later Henry was dead—the victim of a hit-and-run driver?

GILES ABBOTT: His name had appeared with affection in Connie's diaries. But Delia wondered at the expensive watch he wore, and at the strange coincidence involving Giles's grievously ill father . . .

* * *

"Marian Babson's name on a mystery is a guarantee of quality writing wrapped around an unusual crime."

—*Houston Chronicle*

"Babson writes mysteries with distinctive atmosphere, sympathetic characters, and stylish verve."

—*Booklist*

MARIAN BABSON

PAST REGRET

WARNER BOOKS

A Time Warner Company

WARNER BOOKS EDITION

Copyright © 1990 by Marian Babson
All rights reserved.

This Warner Books Edition is published by arrangement with St. Martin's Press, 175 Fifth Avenue, New York, N.Y. 10010.

Cover design by Jackie Merri Meyer
Cover illustration by Phillip Singer

Warner Books, Inc.
1271 Avenue of the Americas
New York, NY 10020

 A Time Warner Company

Printed in the United States of America

First Warner Books Printing: November, 1993

10 9 8 7 6 5 4 3 2 1

CHAPTER 1

Charnel House . . .

In the silence of the night she cocked her head to one side, trying to catch an echo of the words. Where had they come from? Who had said them? What did it have to do with her?

No echo. Nothing but silence. She was alone in the mist, on a deserted street.

It wasn't much of a street. Mostly empty lots. Here and there a lone narrow house, shored-up by elaborate triangular skeleton frames on either side. Houses like stubborn teeth, making a last stand in a rapidly emptying jaw. House . . . charnel house . . .

In the distance, cranes towered against the skyline like giant praying mantises, poised to advance and devour everything in their path. In this area the demolition work had already been done, the rebuilding had not yet started.

She drifted onwards. It worried her to stand still. She felt safer moving. Ahead, the mist was thicker. She moved into it. The mist was safer, too. It blurred everything in a friendly, merciful way.

A solid board fence rose up out of the mist. High. Forbidding. Splattered with garish tattered posters advertising obscure rock groups, horror videos, new releases of singles with suggestive titles by improbably named groups. Charnel House . . . was it the name of a group?

She frowned, trying to read through the dark and the mist. Jagged letters leaped at her, shimmering, quivering in some sort of Dayglo:

IT'S ALL OVER NOW—Die Young & the Lace Shrouds
NO MORE CHANCES—Suicide Patrol
MIDNIGHT MADNESS—The Black Massed Choir
DEATH'S COLD EMBRACE—The Waiting Grave
ACID HOUSE— . . .

Acid House . . . Charnel House . . . She backed away, whimpering softly. She kept backing until the posters advertising their grim wares were blotted out by the mist.

Charnel House . . . not a group. Probably not a group. If only she weren't so tired . . . she could think . . .

She stumbled, but caught herself before falling. Too tired. So tired she hadn't even noticed the curbstone. What else was she missing?

She looked up at the blood-red sky. No, no, not blood! The sky was always red over a city. It was the reflection of all the lights below. She turned her back on the city, moving off in the opposite direction.

So tired . . . she should go home. Home . . . ? Home . . . house . . . charnel house.

What a strange phrase to be haunting her. No, not strange . . . sinister. She shivered, even though the night wasn't that cold. The cold was within her. She was freezing, even though she was wrapped in a big expensive overcoat.

Overcoat? Cashmere . . . black . . . unfamiliar . . . the buttons on the wrong side . . . a man's overcoat. What man? Wouldn't he want it back? Had he gallantly placed it across her shoulders to keep off the dank chill? What had happened to him?

There had been someone else with her when she started out, hadn't there? For an instant, a blur of a face shimmered at the edge of her consciousness, a name hovered just beyond recall.

She couldn't worry about that right now. When she wasn't so tired . . . after a good night's sleep . . . she'd remember. Of course she'd remember.

Sleep . . . where? Home . . . house . . . charnel house . . .

She shivered again and thrust her hands deep into the pockets. There was something in the left-hand pocket. Her fingers explored the strange thick cylinder, turning it round, testing it. Like the overcoat, it was unfamiliar and too big.

Instinctively, she glanced around. She was operating entirely by instinct now, her mind seemed to have deserted her, gone on strike. Against what? Had she been overworking it, treating it badly?

There was an unvandalized streetlamp ahead. She floated towards it casually, without eagerness, to deceive any watchers. Who would be watching? At this hour? In this desolated area?

She paused beneath the dim glow, looked around again, then drew her hand out of the pocket, lifting it up to her face as though looking at her watch. The sleeve was too long, it slid down over her knuckles. She inched her clenched hand out far enough to see what it was clutching . . . and gasped.

A bankroll. Literally. A fat cylinder of rolled banknotes, held by a rubber band. Thick enough to choke a horse. Literally.

Suddenly, she was frightened. She thrust her hand back into the pocket and walked swiftly away from the light. By the time she was safely into the shadows, she was running. Somewhere . . . anywhere . . .

Darker shadows were swooping at her inside her mind, black threatening shapes that would not slow down enough to let her glimpse them. She didn't want to get a closer look at them. She had already seen enough. Too much.

The outside banknote had been a fifty-pound note. She had just been able to discern the five-zero beneath the blur, the red-brown smear over the numbers. Redder-brown than the brown scrolls of the note's engraving. Red-brown, still damp, and faintly sticky to the touch.

The sudden stitch in her side slowed her down. That and the growing dampness. She was near the river. Too near. She stopped. She wasn't ready for the river. Not yet . . .

Exhaustion weighed down on her, but she kept moving. At least she had enough money. She could get a room in a hotel . . . if she could find a hotel. She had to rest . . . to sleep . . . she'd feel better then.

Maybe then she could find her way home. Home . . . house . . . charnel house . . .

CHAPTER 2

"There was no letter again today."

He rustled his newspaper at her. Irritated. Everything she said and did irritated him these days.

"It's been three weeks. Without even a postcard."

"For God's sake, Delia!" The newspaper twitched, revealing one furious eye. "She's young, she's abroad, she's having the time of her life! She doesn't want to be bothered with The Old Folks at Home."

He never called her Dee any more. The use of her full name seemed to distance her in a curious way. And this wasn't the first time he'd made references to her age. *Her* age, was the implication, not his. Women aged, men mellowed.

"You know Connie is the Great Communicator. She's written once a week, sometimes twice, since she's been there *and* often sent a postcard as well. Why should she suddenly stop?"

"She's just having too good a time—"

"Something's wrong, I know it!"

"Don't be so neurotic! Why should anything be wrong? She's busy, that's all. People have their own lives to lead—" His mouth stayed open, as though he would like to add more, but didn't quite dare.

They stared at each other across the chasm that had been widening imperceptibly for months until, abruptly, it was too wide, too deep, to cross.

"You worry too much about those kids," Hal said, as though he had never given her any reason to worry. "They're OK. Just spreading their wings, that's all. They can't spend every minute looking back over their shoulders at the past."

So she was the past now, was she? Her work done, the children raised and set upon their paths into the world, the future. No looking back. Hal wasn't doing much looking back himself lately.

"Look, what could be wrong?" Something in the quality of her silence seemed to unnerve Hal. "You called the college last week, didn't you? And they said everything was all right."

"They didn't say that. They said they were still on their Easter Break and most of the students were off travelling on the Continent."

"There you are! Same thing. Connie's having herself a whale of a time in the sidewalk cafés of Paris, or exploring Amsterdam, or something. She's too busy to write. We'll hear all about it when she gets home."

"She hasn't even sent one postcard. You know that's not like her."

"Maybe it's gone astray. These things happen." He rustled his newspaper, anxious to get back to it. Or just anxious to end the conversation. "You worry too much."

"She should be back at the college by now. I'm going to call again."

"Go ahead, if you must." He retreated behind the newspaper. "You know where the phone is and how to use it."

"It's too late now. It will be three o'clock in the morning in London."

"OK, call tomorrow, then. If it will make you happy." He threw down the newspaper and switched on the television. "Let's catch the news. There must be something happening somewhere in the world—there's nothing in the paper."

Dee didn't bother to answer that. What was happening in her world wasn't being telecast or printed in any newspaper. It was there to be read all over Hal. He had found himself another woman; one who was clearly an old-fashioned girl. For the old-fashioned signals were being posted all over his person: the artfully-draped golden hair on the back of his jacket, the traces of perfume on his lapel, the smudges of coral lipstick on his collar. The woman must think Dee exceptionally stupid, however, for tonight there was an almost complete lipstick print at the back of his collar.

The challenge was implicit: *Try ignoring that!*

Dee ignored it. All the bits of evidence, she had noticed, had been planted where Hal would be unaware of them. That meant the other woman was trying to force them into a confrontation. Hal was being manipulated by her. He wasn't ready for confrontation. Not yet.

"I'll call first thing in the morning," Dee said. She wouldn't need to set the alarm; she hadn't been sleeping much lately.

"Sawyer . . . Constance Sawyer . . . ?" The voice on the other end of the line muttered, sounding far less alert than Dee, although it was nine-thirty in the morning over there and four a.m. for Dee.

"She's one of the American students on the Junior Year Abroad Program," Dee said crisply. Last week she had had this same conversation with some woman; this morning the woman had put her through to this man. She tried to keep the irritation out of her voice, but surely he must know that there had already been an inquiry about

Connie. His vagueness confirmed her suspicion that no one was doing anything about the situation over there.

"Ah yes, here we are." His voice firmed and strengthened. "I'm afraid you can't speak with her at the moment."

"I don't especially want to speak to her, I just want to know if she's there."

"I'm afraid she's unavailable at the moment."

"Is she there?" Dee had begun to hate the smug, cold voice.

"As I have told you—" The voice didn't like her, either. She was obviously being marked down as a troublemaker. "Miss Sawyer is unavailable at the present moment."

"Your classes have started again, haven't they? Your Easter Break is over?"

"Er . . . yes," he admitted reluctantly. "Classes resumed on Monday for the new term. But it's early days yet—"

"Then surely you can tell me whether my daughter is 'unavailable' because she's in class—or because she isn't there at all?" Dee heard her voice rising and had to make a conscious effort to control it. "I'm her mother. I have a right to know."

"I just told you—" A faint desperation shaded the other voice. "It's early days yet. The very beginning of a new term. Quite a few of the students take their time about returning, especially if they've been touring on the Continent, as most of the foreign ones do. We have to allow them a few days' leeway."

"She isn't back," Dee said flatly.

"She's overdue, certainly, but so are a lot of other students. It's nothing unusual at this time of year. They'll all be back at their desks in another week or so. This happens every term."

"My daughter hasn't written to me in three weeks." Dee tried to make him understand the growing urgency of her fear.

"We try—" A martyred sigh drifted over the line. "We remind them constantly to write home, but one cannot stand over each and every one of them and physically force him or her to do so."

His voice was sliding into an aggrieved whine, the voice of a time-server, beset by unreasonable demands and monstrous charges. The voice of a man with one eye on the clock and the other on the calendar, counting out the minutes until early retirement.

"May I have your name, please?"

"My name—what do you want that for?" Panic shaded the voice. Dee could sense that he was mentally reviewing their conversation to see if he'd said anything rude enough to have upset her to the point of reporting him to his superiors.

"I would like to know to whom I am speaking."

"Oh . . ." The pedantic phrasing seemed to reassure him, his voice was more relaxed as he answered. "This is Professor Standfast . . . Professor Justin Standfast."

"Professor Justin Standfast." She didn't need to write it down, she would remember. Standfast—a misnomer if there ever was one. He was the sort of man to cut and run at the first hint of trouble.

"Thank you, Professor Standfast." She decided to give him a hint of the trouble in store, let him worry. "I also want to know whom to ask for when I arrive."

"Arrive? Where? Oh, see here—"

"My daughter is missing, Professor Standfast. That may not worry you, but it worries me. I'll be on the first flight I can get."

CHAPTER 3

Shadows . . . there were shadows all around her. Behind her eyes as well as in front of them. She felt shadowlike herself as she drifted along. Insubstantial . . . but safe . . . safe so long as she kept moving. It wasn't safe to stop. The shadows swooped at her then. Swooped, collided, broke apart into menacing nightmare shapes . . . no, it was safer to keep moving. The shadows couldn't catch up with her that way.

But her feet hurt. She didn't know how long she had been walking. Time was behaving like the shadows, too. It kept advancing and retreating, but also without any real substance or meaning. It was no longer a measurement of anything. When you had nowhere definite to go and no specific hour at which to arrive, time was meaningless.

The shadows thickened and solidified. Night, then, not just shadows. Another night . . . how many had there been?

Her mind winced away from the question. It was not ready for questions yet. Questions were too unsettling . . . too dangerous.

Charnel house . . .

Her mind winced away from that one, too. Winced— and closed down. *No more . . . move on . . . move on . . .*

She had sat down on a bench at a bus stop to rest her feet. She watched a green bus approach on the horizon and move towards her. She lurched to her feet . . . her aching feet. Perhaps it would be better to get on the bus and sit down and be carried along. It didn't matter where the bus was going. Any destination would do.

She waved, although the bus driver had already seen her. The bus was slowing, its directional signal blinking as it pulled over to the stop.

She was glad that she had signalled. The driver had clearly expected it. Why else would a woman be sitting at a bus stop in the middle of nowhere? There was nothing to be seen but fields under cultivation in every direction and night was descending rapidly. If she had motioned him on, he would have wondered to himself, perhaps remembered her. As it was, she would be just another passenger.

Hydraulics hissed as the door opened and she gathered up her bags. Somewhere, she had acquired a satchel-type bag; it was fairly heavy, although she could not remember what she had in it. There was also a plastic shopping-bag; she couldn't remember what was in that, either. They were obviously things she had purchased at some time when the shadows had been thinner . . . when she had passed through some town . . .

"Where to, luv?" the bus driver beamed. A return smile seemed to be indicated.

"End of the line," she whispered, drawing a handful of change from the deep pocket of her overcoat and offering it to him.

"One pound thirty." He helped himself without surprise. It appeared that there was nothing unusual about this, nothing memorable.

She accepted the strip of paper from him with another fleeting smile and made her way to the rear seats. There were not many other passengers and they paid no attention to her.

She settled into the last double seat in front of the long seat that stretched across the back. She put the satchel on the seat beside her to discourage anyone from sitting there in the event that they picked up more passengers along the way. One pound thirty seemed to indicate that they had quite a distance to travel. The shopping-bag she placed on the floor at her feet.

The spurt of activity seemed to have exhausted her. She closed her eyes and relaxed into the comfortable swaying of the bus. Until the shadows came too close . . . grew too black . . . too menacing . . .

Her eyelids flew open—had she been asleep? Her impulse was to look around wildly, but she forced herself to remain still. She could survey the entire bus from where she sat. Almost the entire bus. Moving slowly, she took a cautious look over her shoulder. The rear seat was still unoccupied; nothing had changed while her eyes had been closed.

The feeling of panic gradually subsided, giving way to a mild curiosity. The bags . . . they must be hers . . . they had felt right when she picked them up. What was in them?

The satchel first. She unzipped it and looked inside as though opening a time capsule—or a message from a different self. Someone who had once existed beyond the shadows.

Underclothes . . . a blouse and skirt . . . a nightgown. And a pair of slippers—so inviting, but if she took her shoes off, she might never get them on again. Toothbrush . . . toothpaste . . . soap and washcloth . . . the bare necessities. Why should she need anything more?

The plastic carrier bag at her feet bore the logo of a

chain store. It was filled with newspapers . . . with something heavier at the bottom. She pushed the newspapers aside . . . she didn't want to think about newspapers . . . and dived for the treasure at the bottom.

Treasure! A packaged ham, cheese and pickle sandwich, two cartons of fruit juice with straws, a packet of cookies and two chocolate bars, one with and one without almonds.

Her stomach suddenly convulsed, telling her that it had been without food for far too long. Why? She had bought the food, obviously intending to eat it. What had stopped her? Distracted her? Brought the shadows swooping down around her again, so that the only safety was in flight?

The newspapers? She pulled one out of the bag and tore at the pages, scanning them for something. What? There was nothing disturbing in the first paper. More slowly, she went through the others. Nothing. She could throw them all away now, she had no more need of them.

Right now, she needed sustenance. She shook one of the fruit juice cartons, poked the straw through the little silver circle and took a deep draught. Oh, that was good. It was still faintly chilled, perhaps she had bought it not too long ago.

Urgently, she clawed the covering off the sandwich and took a bite, then another. She was beginning to feel human again. Or almost. There was more to being human than she had been experiencing lately. But she couldn't remember what . . . she couldn't remember . . .

The shadows fluttered at the edges of her consciousness and she concentrated on eating her sandwich. You had to have food. She could remember that much.

Every crumb of the sandwich, every drop of the fruit juice, then the packet of cookies and the other carton of fruit juice— she'd needed that, needed it for a long time. She'd save the chocolate bars until later, they could wait now. When she got to a town again, she would replenish her supplies. It was better to carry emergency rations with you at all times . . . safer.

She would buy more newspapers, too; the latest editions. She piled the newspapers she had finished with neatly on the seat beside her, behind the satchel, preparatory to leaving them there when she got off the bus. She recognized familiarity in the act. She had done it before. She had become a compulsive newspaper-buyer, reading and discarding them quickly when they failed to catch her interest.

She didn't know what she was looking for, but she would know it when she saw it . . .

CHAPTER 4

Half way across the Atlantic—just past the Point of No Return—the favorable tailwinds gave way to turbulence.

Dee clung grimly to the arm-rests and concentrated on trying to keep the plane in the air as it dropped and bucked. It would be too convenient for Hal if she were to die in a plane crash. He and his new love could move on into their rosy future with no ties to the past, no sense of guilt—and no alimony payments hanging over their heads.

And what would become of Connie? It would be a long

time before Hal pulled his head out of the sand and began to wonder where she was. He wouldn't—

"We are in the hands of the Lord." Her seatmate spoke abruptly. "We always are, of course, but times like this make you realize it afresh. We must put our trust in Him."

"Yes," Dee said between clenched teeth. The Lord hadn't been doing very well by her lately. Even her departure had been delayed because all immediate flights had been booked, and then there had been the multiplicity of little things that had to be attended to before she could get away. She was already two days later than she had thought she would be when she spoke to Professor Standfast. By the time they arrived at Heathrow, it would be morning of the third day. And there had still been no word from Connie.

"You're younger." The other woman spoke forgivingly. "You have more to lose. Now me, I lost my dear husband ten years ago, but I feel he's waiting for me somewhere out there—"

The plane bucked again and lost more altitude. One of the engines changed pitch and developed a nasty whine.

"In fact, I feel he's pretty close to me right this minute." Despite the rapt expression on the woman's face, panic flashed in her eyes.

"Mm-hmm . . . " Dee was listening to the penetrating whine. Was the engine going to cut out altogether? How strong were the other engines? Jets were supposed to be able to make it on one engine, but in this kind of turbulence . . . ?

"We'll meet them again, dear," the woman assured her. "They're waiting for us just behind the storm clouds. Your husband, too."

"Mine?" Dee was momentarily so startled that she forgot to will the engine to continued life.

"I hope you don't mind me mentioning it. I couldn't help noticing, I know the look. It was recent, wasn't it? If you don't want to talk about it, I understand. But it's written all over your face, the loss. You have that bereft look—"

"I'm afraid I don't want to talk about it."

"And there was nobody to see you off at the airport. I couldn't help noticing that."

No, Hal hadn't seen her off. He'd be working late, he'd joked—not noticing that he was the only one who thought it funny. Working overtime to pay for her extravagance, for her heedless, unnecessary trip to check up on a child who was too busy to write and would not appreciate the descent of an anxious parent to spoil her fun.

But he wouldn't try to stop her. Oh no, of course he wouldn't. Relief had throbbed in his voice. He was looking forward to his own fun while she was away, to a free run with his mistress, unhampered by the need to report back to base, to invent excuses for staying out late. "Working overtime" had been overworked to the point that it had almost become a joke, would have become a joke were it not for the nagging look of anxiety in his eyes every time he produced it—that and the insistence that she must never, never call him at the office, not even in the direst emergency. He would be too busy to be bothered; she must cope with it by herself until he returned home.

If he returned home. The thought was always at the back of her own mind. Unspoken, because to speak would be to bring it all out into the open, perhaps force a decision, a choice. Hal wasn't ready to make a choice yet. Like most men, he didn't see why things couldn't just go on the way they were. It was the other woman who was forcing the pace; perhaps if she nagged Hal hard enough, he might decide that he preferred the more placid and un-demanding company of his wife.

But did she want him on those terms? Knowing that, if he broke up with this woman, he might go on to find an-other? She wasn't ready to make a decision yet, herself. They were a good pair, she and Hal, united in their avoid-ance of unpalatable truths, clinging to the *status quo*, un-willing to move unless forced into action.

As she had been forced into action now. She could do nothing about Hal, but she could find out what had hap-pened to Connie. The trouble was that, in a traitorous cor-ner of her mind, she halfway agreed with Hal. Perhaps Connie, overwhelmed by new sights, new friends and the kind of freedom she had never experienced before, had just forgotten to write. It was easy to do, one just kept putting it off, not noticing how much time was passing. Obviously, the whole family was adept at putting things off.

Especially Hal Junior. Now that he was away at col-lege, months could pass without a letter—unless his allowance ran out. Fortunately for the state of their com-munications, if not Hal Senior's bank account, the al-lowance ran out regularly, ensuring a monthly letter pointing out the rising cost of living.

It was too bad that Connie was so good at managing her allowance. She had always taken pride in the fact that she had never sent a begging letter, even though she knew her parents wouldn't mind. But she had always been good at writing short chatty letters keeping them up to date with what she called her adventures. That was the chilling thought: had she had one adventure too many?

"It's over now," her seatmate said, for a moment seeming in accord with her thoughts. "We won't meet them this time, dear."

A soft chime punctuated the words and the "No Smoking" signs flicked off. "Fasten Seat-Belt" remained lit; the pilot was taking no chances. There could still be more turbulence ahead.

The cabin staff began moving into view, displaying bright, unconcerned faces, taking orders for drinks. One of the braver—or more desperate—passengers unbuckled his seat-belt and walked purposefully towards the toilets. A hum of conversation and nervous laughter began to rise.

"He was close to us." Her companion seemed determined to continue. "I could feel him waiting for me. Didn't you feel that your dear lost one was standing by to help you cross over?"

"I'm sorry," Dee said. "I'm tired." She closed her eyes firmly and turned her head away.

She wouldn't have believed that she could actually sleep after all that, but exhaustion took over. She awakened to a bustle of activity as breakfast was served to those who were interested. Below them, patches of green dotted a sparkling blue sea. In the distance, a larger island loomed.

Dee gazed down on it bleakly. Not for her the thrill of anticipation being voiced by the other travellers. Whether whatever was waiting for her down there was to be welcomed or feared was something she would find out soon enough.

At least, she hoped she would. The alternative was unthinkable, and yet there were parents who had to live through it, day after day, week after week, month after month, of not knowing what had happened to their child, whether it was alive or dead, lost, strayed or stolen. Hoping, fearing, searching every crowd, wondering if they'd recognize their own child as the years piled up. Connie was grown, almost an adult, but she might still grow another inch or two, gain weight, lose weight, change her hairstyle, dye her hair . . .

So many imponderables, leaving aside the one most dreadful: had Connie disappeared because she wanted to?

The hotel was just off a leafy green square. It was the hotel Connie had recommended, when she had urged her parents to come to England for the Christmas holidays. But Hal had had too much "overtime" during the long holiday season from Thanksgiving through New Year. "You go ahead, Dee," he had said. (She had still been Dee then.) "You and Connie can have a great time without me." She had weighed the possibility, already aware that something was going wrong between them, not sure what, but beginning to suspect. Would it be wise to go away and leave the field clear for some other woman?

And what about Junior? Would it be fair to him to seem to neglect him in favor of his sister? He would be coming home for Christmas, expecting the usual celebration, perhaps expecting a bit of extra attention now that he would be the only chick in the nest. Could she, in fairness, rush off and leave him? What kind of a Christmas would he have, with his father too immersed in his own concerns to want to be bothered with him?

While she was still trying to decide, another letter had come from Connie, excited, enthusiastic—and slightly apologetic. She had been invited to spend the holidays with a friend in the country. Her parents hadn't seemed very keen on the idea of coming over anyway, and Junior

would be lost without them. Besides, the weather would
be so much better in the spring and there would be more
opportunities for side trips, perhaps to the Continent. It
might be more fun if they came over then, or perhaps
later—for the end of the Junior Year Abroad—and perhaps they could travel around for a bit and all go home together.

Would it have made any difference if Dee had gone
over for Christmas?

It was spring now. An early spring here; there was still
snow on the ground in Connecticut. Through the jetlag
haze, Dee had seen the first flowers and blossoming
shrubs of spring in the neat little gardens as her taxi carried her into the heart of the city on the long journey from
Heathrow. It was easier to contemplate the gardens than to
think about the already-frightening size of the city.

Even the size of her hotel room was daunting: high-
ceilinged, French-windowed, with great vaulting spaces
between the small islands of furniture. An enormous mirror almost covered one wall, making the room look even
larger and curiously empty. It cried out to reflect a bevy of
gracious Edwardian beauties in low cut gowns, bustles
and flowing skirts, not one small travel-stained woman in
a rumpled jacket and skirt badly creased from hours of sitting in a cramped airplane seat. She felt as out of place as
a chimney sweep who had stumbled into the ante-room of
a palace.

Yet, on a closer look, the room was not quite what it
seemed. The paint was flaking from the ceiling and there
was a crack in one corner; worn, if not quite threadbare,
patches on the carpet in front of brighter patches where
the pattern showed more clearly betrayed that there had
once been more furniture in the room. The mirror was

streaked with darkness where its silvered backing had tarnished.

Faded grandeur. Strangely, she began to feel more comfortable. She, with her wrinkled skirt, wasn't so out of place after all. They'd all seen better days.

The room was still pleasing, as was the view of the leafy green square from the not-quite-French windows. (They didn't extend all the way to the floor, nor did they open out to give access to what was just a suggestion of a balcony—more of an overgrown window ledge with an iron railing—nothing one would wish to step out on to.)

Dee had just started to unpack when the first wave of exhaustion washed over her, leaving her so weak and dizzy that she had to lean against the wall. The room blurred and faded. She closed her eyes and took several deep breaths; they didn't help much.

She couldn't collapse! Not here, not now. Connie needed her, she knew it. If she fell ill, she would be no use to anyone.

Jetlag, she told herself firmly. It was just jetlag, combined with exhaustion, combined with emotion, with anxiety, with fear . . . Perhaps it was a panic attack; that would hardly be surprising. She had been running scared for a long time now, even before she had begun worrying about Connie.

It was time to start fighting back. That was why she was here. She opened her eyes and pushed herself away from the wall.

The room swayed again. Perhaps it might be the better part of valor to take a nap first. She must be sensible, however much she wanted to rush out and start dashing about in all directions.

She pulled her nightgown and robe from her case. A

deep throbbing ache had begun at the base of her skull and was spreading out, travelling upwards towards her forehead and eyes and downwards through her neck and shoulders. Across the room, the bed looked as inviting as an oasis in the desert. No matter whether it was really comfortable or not, it was a place where she could lie flat and sleep—or perhaps just slide into unconsciousness.

But not yet. One final task loomed ahead of her; the hurdle she must jump first. She looked around and found the telephone. As she dialed, she felt the unquenchable hope rising again. It was possible that Connie was back. The college was into the second week of term now. Connie could have already returned, have telephoned home to apologize for her long silence. Hal would have no way of reaching her to tell her; he wouldn't have bothered to telephone the hotel to leave a message, knowing that she would check with the school again as soon as she arrived. Besides, he had other matters on his mind.

Once she was sure Connie was safe, she could worry about that. Once she had spoken to Connie and seen her. Now that she was here, they could have that holiday together, go to the theater, visit some of the historical sights. Of course, Connie would still have to attend classes, but perhaps she could cut just a few. They might even take a short trip to Paris; it would be silly to come all this way and never see Paris. Hope was in control now, soaring higher, as the half-formed plans began to take shape in her mind.

"Hello . . . hello . . . ?" The woman's voice was sharp with growing annoyance, as though suspecting an obscene caller. "Is anyone there?"

"I'm sorry," Dee apologized quickly. "Good morning. I'd like to speak to Connie—Constance—Sawyer, please."

In the long silence before the other woman answered, hope fluttered and died.

"I'm sorry, she's not available right now. Would you like to leave a message?"

"No . . . " Dee said slowly. "No message."

"Wait—" the woman called. "Who is this? Why do you want to speak to Miss Sawyer?" There was a note of uneasiness in her voice.

"No message," Dee repeated softly and replaced the receiver.

CHAPTER 5

As soon as she woke she knew that this was going to be one of her good days. In their way, they were worse than the bad days.

On a bad day she walked in a merciful haze, content just to get through the day. Without questions, without worries, one step after another, like a zombie, no problems. Zombies didn't have problems. It was all over for them; they were the living dead. So, on a bad day, was she.

Even so, the good days were more disturbing. It was then that she knew—or suspected—how much she did not know. It was then that the questions began to surface in her consciousness. Questions she could not answer.

With the questions came the fears she could not explain. And the anxieties about the future.

On the bad days she didn't know what the word future meant. On the good days she knew that she had one—such as it might be. She also knew that she had no past. That was more frightening than anything.

Amnesia. She wasn't stupid, she knew the word for her condition. On the good days. What she didn't know was what she could do about it. Or how it had come about. Among the strange nuggets of information she had discovered when rummaging through her mind, was the fact that amnesia was usually the result of a blow to the head, possibly received in an automobile accident.

She had sat for a long time, pondering that knowledge. It seemed intellectually correct, yet it had nothing to do with her emotionally. She did not *feel* that she had been in a car accident. Yet she could remember little else, so why should that memory not have eluded her also?

But she didn't *look* as though she had been in an accident, either. There were no cuts or bruises anywhere on her body. She had probed her head delicately with her fingers and found no bump or sensitive area. Surely there would have been some physical evidence if she had been in an accident?

Unless it had happened so long ago that the cuts had healed, the bruises faded, the sensitive spot returned to normal. Had she stumbled in a mental fog through that many bad days? She supposed it was remotely possible.

Remote . . . everything was so remote now. Everything she wanted to know seemed to shimmer just beyond the edges of her consciousness and, when she reached out towards it, it disappeared.

And yet, wasn't it creeping a little closer each time?

During the best moments of a good day, she could convince herself that it was. Later, another little chunk of unsuspected knowledge told her that, in some cases, the memory of the final moments before the accident never returned. Some people carried a mental blank of minutes, hours, days, around with them for the rest of their lives.

Other people never remembered anything at all. Ever.

Good day or bad day, that thought was more than she wanted to face. She looked around the room instead.

It was a small room in a large hotel, but it had its own bath and facilities. That was one of the things she had learned. You could be anonymous in a large hotel. In a small, but cheaper, guest house, proprietors were too ready to be friendly, to ask questions. If you had to go down the hall to the bathroom, there were too many chances that you might be intercepted. A regular hotel might be more expensive, but it was worth it in the long run.

Only . . . Another worry surfaced: how much longer would her money last? It had seemed like an enormous amount when she first saw it, but the roll of banknotes was dwindling slowly, inevitably.

And there was something else she did not want to think about. What would happen if—when—she got down to the last few notes? The notes that had been on the outside of the roll when she discovered it, before she had turned the roll inside out so that the smeared notes were hidden at the end, the last ones she would spend. If she dared. Was it her imagination, or were they really bloodstained?

If so, would other people recognize bloodstains if she tried to pass the notes? She had already noticed that shopkeepers scrutinized the fifty-pound notes a lot more closely than they did the tens or twenties.

No, it was too dangerous to risk. But what if—when—she had used all the other notes, she had to use the . . . tainted ones? How could she answer any questions? How could she explain to anyone, when she couldn't even explain it to herself?

She began to wish that it had been one of her bad days. All these questions didn't arise then.

And there were still the biggest questions of all. A curious hum began at the back of her mind, as though to drown them out:

Who am I? Where did I come from? What have I done?

CHAPTER 6

At last she was face-to-face with Professor Justin Standfast.

If you could call it a face. His features were nondescript, to put it at its kindest. But she didn't feel like being kind—not about him. He had the face and bearing of a nonentity.

Pale watery blue eyes shifted rapidly and constantly, refusing to meet her own. Strands of thinning sandy hair streaked across a pale pink scalp. His suit was rumpled and his shirt was faintly grubby.

Making a visible effort, he forced himself to touch her hand—much too briefly to be a handshake—and pulled his own hand back as though it had been burned.

"Ah yes, Mrs. Umm . . . " he said.

"Mrs. Sawyer," Dee said crisply. "As in Constance Sawyer."

"Mrs. Sawyer, do sit down." He scuttled behind the protection of a large mahogany desk, then looked down at it uncertainly. He looked up at her again, then seemed to regret it. She was still there.

"Professor Standfast—" Dee tried to keep the irony out of her voice as she spoke his name, there was no point in antagonizing him at this stage. "Professor Standfast, I do not want to sit down. I want to find my daughter!"

"Ah. Yes." He looked around the office wildly, as though expecting Connie to materialize from behind the looming file cabinets. "Yes, well, it wasn't necessary for you to come all the way over here. The college will take care of all that—if we deem it advisable."

"And when might that be?"

"It is far too early to panic—"

"Maybe for you. But I'm her mother!"

"Quite." He permitted himself a small superior smile. "You are not accustomed to dealing with the vagaries of students *en masse*. We face this little difficulty at the start of every term. It tends to be particularly acute with the foreign students, especially, if I may say so, the transatlantic ones. I suppose that being so close to the famous scenes of history goes to their little heads—"

"How much longer?"

"What—?" Interrupted in mid-flow, he blinked at her accusingly.

"Just how much longer do you propose to stall around before you notify the police that one of your students is missing? The sooner they know, the sooner they can begin finding her."

"No, no." He seemed pained. "I've been trying to explain. Not missing. Just overdue returning to her studies. And she's by no means the only one, I can assure you."

"How many more do you have missing?" Dee challenged.

"Not missing," he insisted. "Absent. On the first day of term, there were ten absent. Two returned by midweek. Then one rang to say that her aunt was visiting from New Zealand and she was taking an extra week for a family holiday. Just this morning another one's mother rang to say that her son had 'flu and wouldn't be back for a few more days. There are now only six— including your daughter—who are absent. Or, should I say, playing truant?" He sighed deeply. "Christmas Break is bad enough, but it's always worst at Easter. The onset of Spring Fever, one presumes."

"So, you have six students . . . absent . . . and you're into the second week of your term. Doesn't that bother you at all?"

His furtive hostile glance told her that she was bothering him far more. He toyed nervously with a silver-framed photograph on the desk: a pleasant-looking woman flanked by two pre-teenage girls with an older boy standing behind her. Fortunately for them, they resembled their mother; there was no trace of Professor Standfast in their happy outgoing features. Perhaps you had to deal with students *en masse* before the iron entered your soul.

"It's early days yet." Reluctantly, he broke the lengthening silence. "By the end of the week, I promise you, we'll have everyone present and accounted for." He spoiled it by adding uneasily. "Or the beginning of next week."

She knew that he must feel her staring at him, for he refused to look up and meet her gaze. His hand moved out towards the photograph again, then twitched away. Perhaps she could appeal to him through his family.

"What if it were *your* daughter?" she asked desperately. "How would you feel if she disappeared without a word? Or your son?"

"I don't have any children," he said huffily, as though she should have known. "I'm not married."

"Oh, but—" Disconcerted, she glanced at the photograph.

"Ah!" He was watching her now. "I see what's confused you. No, they're nothing to do with me. They're Dean Abbott's family. This is the Dean's office. I'm the Acting Dean."

"I see." That explained a lot. He was probably a perfectly useful second-in-command, but not one to initiate action or take on any responsibility.

"In that case—" she had not come all this way to be fobbed off with subordinates— "I want to speak to Dean Abbott."

"I'm sorry, that isn't possible." He enjoyed using his brief authority to thwart her. She began to suspect that she ranked just below troublesome students in his mind. Or perhaps above them.

"Why not? Don't tell me Dean Abbott is still on vacation, too?"

"Would that he were. "No—" he shook his head regretfully. "I'm afraid the Dean is in hospital, very seriously ill."

"I'm sorry." Dee gave the expected reply, although her only sorrow was that she would have to continue to deal with Professor Standfast. "What's wrong?"

"He had a stroke. About three weeks ago. He's been in intensive care ever since. They tell us the fact that he's still alive is something of a wonder, but they aren't holding out much hope of a complete recovery." Professor Standfast looked around the office complacently. Once more his hand stretched out to the family photograph. Without appearing to notice what he was doing, he turned it face down on the desk.

He was so smug, so wrapped up in his own growing importance. He was hardly aware of Dee as a person, certainly not as a mother with a right to be fearful for her daughter's safety, haunted by the terrifying things that could happen to an unprotected young woman in a foreign country. She was just a nuisance to him; worse, a troublemaker. Someone who might endanger his sinecure. It would not look well for an Acting Dean to lose a group of his students almost as soon as he had assumed the post.

He was contemptuous of those students, too. With their "little heads" and "Spring Fever," they were just another source of annoyance. How had a man with so little sympathy for young students risen to such a position of power over them?

Academic politics, presumably. Professor Standfast had the look of one who would do well at the in-fighting, an expert at back-stabbing, poisonous comments, sly remarks that undermined his opponents. He was probably good at paperwork; that sort usually was, preferring paper to people. Paper couldn't answer back. Paper couldn't rock the boat.

She was going to rock it now.

"I'm going to the police," she said. "I'm reporting Connie as a missing person."

"As you wish." His glance conveyed a nicely-judged mixture of acrimony and indifference. "You realize they'll check with the college before they take any action. I shall have to tell them what I have told you. I am more experienced in the ways of the foreign students. They may prefer to be guided by my recommendations in the matter."

"You mean you'd deliberately block an investigation!"

"I would prefer to save the taxpayer unnecessary expense, but, no, I would not 'block an investigation,' as you say." He regarded her thoughtfully. "*If* Constance *is* missing, have you any idea of the complexity of the situation?"

Had she? She had thought of nothing else.

"The police won't have much to go on," he pointed out. "*If* she disappeared, it was during the Easter Break. You won't be able to tell them exactly when she disappeared, when she was last seen, what she was wearing—" He broke off, sighing deeply at the enormity of the problem.

"The trail is cold," Dee acknowledged. "It's too bad you don't take better care of your students."

"My good woman!" He flung his hands in the air. "We are not speaking of children—however juvenilely they may behave. The Junior Year Abroad students are all eighteen years of age or older. Legally—and I never approved of lowering the age from twenty-one to eighteen, the Law is incapable of understanding how emotionally immature so many of them can still be at that age—they are adults. We do what we can, but they must take responsibility for their own lives."

A very convenient attitude. She did not quite dare to say it aloud; she might need his help in the future. After he had finally admitted that Connie was missing.

Her steady gaze seemed to unnerve him. She might as well have said the words aloud; he had sensed them anyway.

"All right! All right!" He flapped his hands at her,

shooing her away. "Do what you want! You will anyway. I can't stop you. But don't blame me for the attitude the police take towards you!"

CHAPTER 7

This was her second night in the same small hotel. Too long, too long. She had to keep moving. It wasn't safe to stay too long in one place. Already, the desk clerk had tried to start a conversation when she had come in at a quiet moment. He was pleasant and probably not much older than she was. (How old was she? How strange not to know.)

She shouldn't have snubbed him quite so firmly. It was dangerous. Now he would remember her—at least for a while. It would have been better to have paused and chatted for a few minutes. What did it matter? She was leaving in the morning anyway. Probably he had just been trying to make a guest feel at home.

At home . . . home . . . house . . .

She pulled her thoughts away. There was no point in letting them stray down that path—it was a dead end.

That was the trouble. There were too many dead ends. Her whole life was a dead end. That was why she could not trust herself to make conversation with anyone.

It had been difficult enough when she checked in. She had already decided to use the name Trent; she had seen it on a street sign and it seemed as good a name as any other. C. Trent. Somehow, the C seemed right.

She had been unprepared for the desk clerk to ask her what the C stood for.

"Co—Co—" she had stammered with rising excitement. She almost had it. Then it slipped away. "Cora," she had finished lamely, remembering another sign: Coral Bookmakers.

At least, she had thought wryly, he would remember her as a girl with a stammer. Also rich—or so he'd imagined. She'd seen the flicker of his eyelids when, aware that she would be asked to pay in advance, she'd produced the fifty-pound note she held in readiness.

"That will be for two nights, then," he had said.

"Yes," she had agreed, afraid to make herself conspicuous in any way. Later, when he'd tried to chat her up, she'd seen the flash "Rich bitch!" in his eyes as she snubbed him.

No, she'd leave in the morning, early—before he came on duty—and move on somewhere else. Where? Did it matter?

Well, yes. Too small a town and people might be too friendly. Too curious. She had already noticed that her accent wasn't quite like everyone else's, but she was a good mimic and could sound like the rest of them—provided she stuck to monosyllables or short sentences. She could not sustain the imitation over a prolonged conversation. It was not just a matter of vowels, it was a different rhythm of speech patterns. If people felt they were beginning to know her, they might feel free to ask her about it. And she didn't know the answer herself.

No, a city then. Not London! She flinched away from the thought in instinctive revulsion. Not London . . .

Another city, there were enough of them. She tried some of the other place names she had garnered from reading the newspapers—if she hadn't known them already. Manchester, Birmingham, Glasgow, Edinburgh, Bristol . . . None of them gave her that same shudder of revulsion. They were all right. It was only London . . .

She shivered violently again. There was something about London . . .

Forget it! Forget it—or sink back into the blankness. She didn't want that. It might be bad enough being conscious of her mental condition, it was worse to be back in the darkness. It could be more dangerous, too. Who knew what might happen if she kept wandering around the way she had been doing? At least, now she was beginning to realize that there was one place she must avoid. Perhaps there were more places. It would be terrible if she were to stumble inadvertently into one of them.

She was stronger, she was definitely stronger—she had to hang on to that. Whether her memory would return with the rest of her strength was something that only time would tell. Meanwhile, she was young, fairly strong and reasonably healthy. She had the rest of her life before her.

The thought had stopped being so frightening now. That was the way it was and she had to face up to it. She had to begin making plans for . . . for going on.

Today is the first day of the rest of your life. The thought sprang into her mind, along with the knowledge that it was a quotation. She couldn't identify the source, but she shrugged off the feeling that she ought to be able to. What was one lost quotation when so much else had been lost?

Let's look on the bright side, Cora. She began taking stock of her invisible assets:

She had a name now, at least. She was Co—Cora Trent.

It was as good a name as any other. Except, perhaps for the one she had lost.

She had the address she had invented for the hotel register. That, too, was adequate. People just wanted the assurance that you had a home address . . . a permanent residence. They never bothered to check up on it. Some employers never even checked references—that would be the kind of employer to find.

Employer . . . yes. She found the decision had been made unconsciously, but she knew that it was the right one. Her money— *was* it hers?—was dwindling away. There was still quite a lot left, but it would not last for ever. Certainly not for the rest of her life. There were many long years ahead of her—unless she was exceptionally unlucky.

Some people might consider that a foregone conclusion. It was not a lucky thing to lose your past.

Or was it? That might depend on what your past had been like— and she was in no position to say.

Still, her present position was not so bad. It could be worse— it *had* been worse. She was *compos mentis* most of the time now. And if her mind wasn't what it had been, who was to know? Unless she chose to tell them. And she was not about to do that.

Never! The consequences upon doing so might be too appalling. That was how she had rationalized her decision not to go to the police. She had never given that possibility serious consideration. It had simply occurred to her as an option, perhaps it was something she had been taught in that lost childhood. If lost, go up to the nearest policeman and tell him you were lost. If you were able to provide him with your name and address, so much the better, but it was not strictly necessary. He would help you. You can always trust a policeman.

Can you? Sometimes adulthood brought different lessons. Had she learned one personally? How maddening to have a brain that presented her with these endless questions without also providing the wherewithal to answer them.

Even if the police were kind and helpful, what could they do? Scan their computers to find out if someone had reported her missing? *Was* there anyone to worry about her whereabouts? Perhaps she was an orphan. She let the possibility echo through her mind, hoping it might provoke a response. Nothing happened.

Or perhaps the police would take her fingerprints and discover that they had them on file. If she had a police record, did she want to know about it? Better to start with a completely clean slate.

There was a final possibility she did not wish to contemplate. They might take her photograph and release it to the newspapers. She would look out at the world from above a caption asking: DO YOU KNOW THIS WOMAN?

And who would come forward to claim her?

Unthinkable! No, she was better off as she was. No police, no publicity. She would go it alone. Start over and see what happened.

It was a challenge. How many people got the chance to re-invent themselves?

CHAPTER 8

Dee Sawyer returned to her hotel room seething with rage. Professor Justin Standfast had tried to make her feel like a fool. The police had succeeded.

The policeman behind the desk had looked down at her with amiable tolerance, as though she were some eccentric who had come in to report that Martians had set up housekeeping in her airing cupboard or the people next door were beaming gamma rays through the wall to give her headaches and frighten the cat.

Her daughter was missing? How old was the girl? Nineteen. Mm. How long had she been missing? Oh, Madam was not quite sure. Three weeks, or possibly four—the last letter to reach Madam in the States had taken six days to arrive; the girl could have disappeared on the day she posted the letter.

Why did Madam believe the girl was missing? Because she had not written again in three weeks. His interest had begun to wane, but not his tolerance. So Madam had flown over from the States on the basis of that, had she? For a moment, his interest sharpened again: Had Madam any reason to suspect foul play? No? No, say, ransom demand? No? The family hadn't enough money to make it worth anyone's while.

"My daughter is missing! She has been missing since classes broke up for Easter. I want you to find her!"

Easter Break—school holiday? Ah, that put a different

complexion on it. Students went travelling on their holidays, either alone or in groups. Had Madam talked to the school authorities about this? Yes? And what did they say? Oh. What was left of his interest evaporated. His patience was slipping, too. He had looked over his shoulder, as though seeking reinforcements from some of the others in the open area of desks behind him, but all heads were bent over their desks to give the impression of being deeply immersed in their own work. Dee had also received the impression that some of them were concealing smiles.

Dee had produced a photo of Connie but that, too, met with a lukewarm response. When had the picture been taken? At a barbecue last Fourth of July. That was almost a year ago. Madam had nothing more recent? A shame, girls can change their appearance so much, grow restless with the same hairdo—or even color.

Was he going to do anything? Her temper snapped. Or wasn't he?

Madam mustn't put it like that. There wasn't much they could do. The girl was an adult—and adults had a right to disappear if they wanted to.

And if they didn't want to? If something had happened to them?

Ah well, that remained to be seen, didn't it? Most people who disappeared returned of their own free will before the year was out. As they had told her at the school, it was early days yet. Especially as her daughter wasn't the only truant. A good sign, that. It was quite likely a group of them had gone off somewhere and were having such a good time that they hadn't noticed so much time had passed. Or did the young lady have a boyfriend? Perhaps she was off with him.

There had been a boyfriend of sorts in the States, several of them, but over here Dee didn't know. Connie hadn't mentioned anyone special in her letters.

Ah, perhaps that meant there was someone very special indeed. It often did.

Dee had fought to control her temper. She could not charge around this city alienating everyone who might be able to help her. "Can't you do anything?" she had pleaded.

They would place Connie on their Missing Persons file and notify Madam if any information came in.

"And then it will be circulated to all other districts," she prodded hopefully.

"Unfortunately no, Madam. There are fifty-two individual police forces throughout the United Kingdom. It wouldn't be practical to circulate—"

"That's terrible!"

"It's unsatisfactory, yes. You might like to place your daughter on record with the Missing Persons Bureau at New Scotland Yard—but they only investigate if the case is thought to involve serious crime. You don't really think that, do you?"

"I don't know. It . . . it might. I don't want to believe that. Connie—"

"Quite so, Madam. Give it a bit more time, why don't you?"

"I can't believe this is all you're going to do. That you won't—"

"We can't, Madam. The young woman is of age. Now, if she had been a child, up to the age of nine or so, we could put out a National Alert. But we can't do that with an adult. Not unless she's a 'vulnerable adult.' I mean—"

he answered Dee's puzzled look—"she isn't elderly. Would you say that she was . . . unstable?"

"Certainly not!" Dee snapped.

"I had to ask," he said. "But that's it, then. She's an adult; it's not an offense to go missing. We can't go making a fuss about it. She might come back from a trip with her boyfriend and be very angry with us. And with you. It could get quite nasty, Madam."

"It's nothing like that. I know it."

The twitch of his eyebrow told her that parents always knew that. And that they were usually wrong.

Stalemate. They stared at each other across the abyss, recognizing each other's point of view, but unable to do anything to change it.

Dee turned away.

"If you find a more recent picture of her, you might drop it in," he said pityingly to her departing back.

Where do you turn for help when the most obvious sources are closed to you? The college refused to admit that there was a problem at all. The police were unable to do anything unless a serious crime was suspected. Please, God, not that!

Sometimes people appealed to the newspapers for help. Hal would be furious—all that publicity! She shrank from it herself. And the policeman was right. Connie would be upset, too, if—when—she returned, to discover that such a hue and cry had been raised for her. No, newspapers, all media, were out . . . except as a last resort.

She had never felt so alone. She hovered irresolutely over the telephone, checking her watch and doing a mental calculation as to the time back home. Even if she called, would Hal be there? Or would he be off somewhere with his new love? How easy it was for men to slough off their old life, like a snake changing its skin. Off with the old life, the old wife, the old family—on with the new.

She had better get used to feeling alone. To being alone.

She turned away from the telephone. She opened her suitcase and took out the thin packet of Connie's letters. She had brought them with her, knowing that Hal would not even notice they were missing. If he did, he would not particularly care. Connie was part of the old life he was in the process of putting behind him. Connie had been written off, along with her mother.

Dee sank into the armchair and began reading the letters again from the beginning, the day after Connie's arrival in England. She had read them so often she had practically memorized them. To start with, she had devoured them to share vicariously in Connie's "adventures." Now she was searching them for clues. Now, so insidious were the policeman's suspicions, she was screening them for veiled references to love and boyfriends. Or boys who were friends at the moment of Connie's writing, but were also prospective lovers.

But she could not settle to read. A raging restlessness was upon her, driving her to toss the letters to one side and begin pacing the room.

Connie was out there somewhere, perhaps alone and in trouble. How could she find her?

On the way back to the hotel, she had stopped at a newspaper shop and picked up a selection of newspapers and a street guide to London. She retrieved the guide from the pile of newspapers and began flipping through it. It was dismayingly thick, page after page of closely diagrammed maps, the names in such tiny print that those of the densely populated districts were barely legible. London was a giant maze of avenues, streets, circles, roads, closes, squares, alleys and turnings, ranging over twenty-five square miles. And she had to face it, Connie might not be in London at all.

She hurled the A-Z from her. It hit the floor with a discouraged plop, an audible counterpoint to her mood. After a moment, she picked it up again. She could not stay in this room another minute. Some action—any action—was preferable.

She had to make a start somewhere. She found Connie's last letter and checked the return address, then looked it up in the A-Z. The place was not far from here. Connie had left her Hall of Residence in order to share a flat with three of her friends. Hal had not liked the idea, neither had she, but there was nothing they could do. The move was already a *fait accompli* by the time Connie wrote to them about it. She would start with Connie's friends.

CHAPTER 9

Coram's Mews turned out to be an alley. The first sight of it produced a sinking feeling in Dee. It looked like the sort of place where muggers might lurk and accidents wait to happen. And she was seeing it at its best in the pale late afternoon sunlight. Instinctively she knew that when darkness fell, only one of the three ancient streetlamps would be working—if that.

No. 5 was halfway down the Mews. A scattering of glass fragments beneath the streetlamp opposite it confirmed her worst suspicions. This was the deepest, darkest part of the Mews. She shuddered to think of Connie walking down this cobbled alley late at night. It couldn't be safe.

The flat was over a disused garage. The whole Mews appeared to be made up of a double row of garages, most of them abandoned, with broken windows and FOR SALE signs hanging dispiritedly over sagging wooden doors.

What was the college thinking of to let young women students leave the protection of their Hall of Residence for a dump like this? If they were thinking at all. Perhaps Professor Standfast had been in charge for longer than she had supposed.

Worse, the narrow street door beside the overswinging garage door was ajar. A flight of rickety stairs led up to No. 5A over the garage. Dee mounted them and was relieved to find that the inner door, at least, appeared to be closed and locked. Somewhat to her surprise, the doorbell was working and she could hear the sharp peal on the other side of the door.

She waited, looking around the cramped passageway. The paint was peeling everywhere; it would be a surprise if it wasn't. But what were those dark furry patches growing up from the floorboards? There was a faint smell of damp and mould pervading the atmosphere.

They were a long time answering the doorbell. Perhaps nobody was home. Dee rang the doorbell again, hope rising. This time she was aware of a slight rustle of sound on the other side of the door, something hit against it with a soft thump.

Impatiently, Dee rang again.

"Who is it?" a voice called cautiously.

"Mrs. Sawyer. I'm Connie's mother."

There was a gasp of consternation, a rattling of the lock and slowly the door swung open. A tall, thin girl stood looking at her gravely, half-defensively.

"How do you do, Mrs. Sawyer. I'm Tanya." She extended her hand, at the same time executing a peculiar back-kick with one foot. "Do come in."

"Thank you." The door opened directly into the living-room. As she entered, Dee saw that the peculiar footwork had not been some sort of suggestion of a curtsey, as she had thought, but an attempt to restrain an exuberant puppy who was frisking around Tanya's feet. He attempted to dart forward to greet Dee.

"I'm sorry." Tanya caught him by the collar and pulled him back. "He's very young. I'm still training him."

"Isn't he quiet?" It was disconcerting to see such a bouncing, healthy puppy who was only making slight squeaking sounds instead of yelping or barking.

"He's a Basenji, they don't bark. My parents said not to get a dog that might disturb the neighbors."

"The neighbors?" Dee glanced towards the deserted Mews.

"Not here." Tanya flushed. "At home. We live in a block of flats. He's a very good guard dog, though," she added defensively.

"You mean, he doesn't bark, he just bites."

"Well, yes. Or he will when I'm through training him. Oh, but he wouldn't bite *you*—" She put her hand on Dee's arm and said firmly. "Friend, Barney, friend." The puppy agreed with a joyous gurgle, wagged his curly tail, and renewed his efforts to reach Dee.

"It's all right." Dee crouched and extended a hand to him. He sniffed at it eagerly and Tanya relaxed her hold on his collar.

"How long have you had him?" Dee asked. "Connie hasn't mentioned him in any of her letters."

"Just over a week. Connie hasn't seen him yet." Tanya flushed unhappily. "I got him while she was gone. I don't think she'll mind."

"Where *is* Connie?" Dee rose to her feet, abruptly ending the social part of the encounter.

"I—I don't know. I mean—" Tanya contradicted herself instantly. "I mean, she's on holiday. We're expecting her back any minute now." She looked towards the door, as though Connie might materialize there at any second.

"When did you last hear from her—any of you?"

"We haven't heard. We didn't expect to. I mean, it was holiday time for all of us. There was no point in sending each other postcards when no one was going to be here to receive them."

Dee looked at her thoughtfully. The girl was more upset than her words indicated. Was it because she knew—or suspected—more than she was admitting?

"Where are the others? I'd like to speak to them, too."

"They're not here just now."

"I can see that." More accurately, she could sense it. The two doors opening off the living-room were ajar and no sound came from behind them. There was no door separating the room from the tiny kitchen, and a narrow door at the back of the kitchen must lead either to the bathroom or to the rear exit—if any. Dee did not get the feeling that any laws regarding fire safety were closely observed in these flats; there might be no back escape route at all.

"I'm just here now because I have a rotten cold." Tanya sniffed unconvincingly. "I decided to cut classes today."

"What time do you expect the others? Did—" Dee groped for their names— "did Jaycee and Maggie go to classes today?"

"I—I'm not sure." This line of questioning was making Tanya very unhappy. "They might have."

"And they might not." Dee watched Tanya trying to think of a satisfactory response.

"I don't know." Tanya shrugged, admitting defeat. "I haven't seen them . . . lately."

"What do you mean by 'lately'?" Dee pounced on the word. "When did you see them last? Before the Easter Break?" The girl's expression told her she was hitting uncomfortably close to the truth. "They haven't come back, either, have they?"

"They—they said they might be back late. They asked me to cover for them."

"And Connie? Did she plan to overstay her break? Were you supposed to cover for her, too?"

"Oh, Mrs. Sawyer—" Tanya was close to tears. "I'm sorry. I wish I could tell you she did, but she didn't. I don't know what's happened to—I mean, I don't know where she is or why she isn't back. I've been getting so worried."

"That makes two of us." Dee reflected grimly that it was too bad that the other half of the worried duo couldn't have been Hal. But it was too late to worry about that now.

"Are they together?" Dee snapped.

"What? Who?"

"Did Connie go off with Jaycee and Maggie?"

"Oh no!" Tanya seemed shocked. "She wouldn't do that!"

"Why not?" There was something funny here.

"Well, um, she just wouldn't. She's more tactful than that. They—they had reservations made for just the two of them."

"The two of *them*," Dee echoed thoughtfully.

"Oh!" Tanya appeared quite relieved as the telephone rang. "Excuse me, I'll have to answer the phone."

She was nervous as she crossed the room under Dee's watching gaze. "Sit down," she said uneasily. "Please. I won't be a minute."

Unhappily for Tanya, the telephone was in a corner of the living-room. She picked it up and compromised with privacy by half-turning her back on Dee. "Hello?" The response made her even unhappier.

"Oh, hello, Dr. Carson. Yes, this is Tanya. No, I'm sorry, er, Jaycee isn't here right now. No, I don't know when he'll be back . . . "

He? Jaycee was a male? Dee stopped listening. Connie hadn't told them that. Not surprisingly. She'd have known her father would have thrown a fit—and her mother wouldn't be very pleased, either. Connie hadn't been guilty of an outright lie, but it was a definite deception. By referring to Jaycee by name, Dee realized now, and never by gender, Connie had allowed her parents to assume that Jaycee was another girl; that four females were sharing the flat. She had intended them to assume that.

What else hadn't Connie told them? What other little deceptions was she involved in?

Tanya was still placating Dr. Carson, reluctant to end one awkward conversation and go back to another. Even after replacing the receiver, she hesitated to turn around.

The soundless puppy skittered around her feet, inviting her with chuckles and wheezes to stop what she was doing and play with him. The click of his claws on the bare floorboards made more noise than came from his throat.

Dee waited.

"I'm sorry." Tanya stooped to calm the puppy, keeping her face hidden. "That was Dr. Carson—Jaycee's tutor. He's missed another tutorial. I—I'm sure he never intended to miss so many. I thought they were just going to be gone a few extra days. I—I just don't know what to tell Dr. Carson."

"Isn't it about time you started telling everyone the truth?"

"I've told you the truth." Tanya looked up, startled.

"Yes, I suppose you have. I'm sorry." It was Connie who had been deceitful; she shouldn't vent her anger on this innocent girl. "What I mean is, isn't it time you reported this situation to the college authorities? Tell them that your flatmates are missing—"

"They're not missing!" Tanya cried. "They'll be back."

"They're overdue now," Dee pointed out. She marvelled to herself at the traumatic effect the word "missing" had on English people. Tanya was every bit as horrified by it as Professor Standfast had been; like him, she was denying the implications it carried. Dee had felt like that herself initially; she had had time to get used to the word, to steel herself to the implications.

"You were expecting them all back before this, weren't you?"

"Yes," Tanya admitted, on the verge of tears. The puppy pricked up his ears and whined softly in sympathy. "I went home for the holiday, so I wasn't here when they left. I knew I was supposed to cover for them for a few days, then for a few more days I thought something might have delayed them—a ferry strike or airport problems or something. I've been expecting them every day."

"You said they weren't together."

"Jaycee and Maggie were. They're living together. That's why they moved out of the Residences, so that they could. They found this flat, but they couldn't swing it alone, so Connie and I joined them to help with the rent and share expenses."

"I see." Another part of the deception.

"I keep hoping they'll come back soon," Tanya said despairingly. "Every day I think: surely they'll be here when I get back from classes. But they're not."

"Meanwhile, you're here all alone."

"I have Barney." The pup looked up and wriggled happily at the sound of his name. "He's really quite a good watchdog already."

Dee looked at her: a frightened but fiercely proud girl, alone in this ramshackle building, guarded by a puppy who couldn't bark and still had his milk teeth. Dee sighed deeply.

"Sit down, Tanya," she said. "We've got to talk this through."

CHAPTER 10

She was proud of herself. Her first day's pay, here in her hand. The first money she had ever earned—that she knew of. And it had been quite easy, after all. Not strictly legal, perhaps, but easy.

From somewhere deep inside herself she had plucked the knowledge that casual catering staff were always needed—no questions asked. Cash would be paid in hand at the end of each day and work was on a day-to-day basis, especially during busy seasons.

It promised to be endlessly fascinating, discovering all these buried nuggets of arcane information she possessed. Like rummaging through an attic on a rainy afternoon, unearthing all sorts of unregarded treasure.

"We're going to do all right, Co—Cora," she murmured to herself. It pleased her to know that she could live frugally for a couple of days on her earnings, especially as a good meal had been part of the arrangement. Maybe she would risk going back to the restaurant and working there again tomorrow.

No longer than that, though. Not with the speculative way the proprietor had been looking at her. Not after he had muttered that the day after tomorrow was his wife's day off—and there could be time-and-a-half for overtime.

Some things you didn't have to dive very deeply into your psyche to know about.

But one more day ought to be safe and it would help

her to get back into the swing of things. Then she must be on her way again. Where didn't matter. When you had no home, all places were alike—or something like that. Dimly she recognized another quotation, or a bit of one. It didn't matter.

When real solid survival-type information had been needed, her mind had come through for her. That was what counted.

What counted, too, was that she was stronger physically. Probably she hadn't been eating very well during what she had come to think of as "the lost days." She wondered how many there had been, then wondered if she really wanted to know.

She had been deeply—almost mortally—wounded. In the mind, instead of the body, and she must recognize that it was going to take a long time to recover. She had to face the fact that she might never recover completely, that most, if not all, of her previous life was missing as surely as an amputated limb. If she kept reminding herself of that, eventually it might not seem so frightening.

Spending these few days in the same place had helped, crystallizing the knowledge that she needed a long quiet period of rest now. She had been on the run for too long. She needed to go to ground somewhere, lie low . . .

The sudden unpredictable uneasiness welled up from her subconscious. She had told herself, convinced herself, that she must consider herself as an invalid—a recovering invalid. Why then did she persist in thinking like a fugitive?

"Spending." Was that the trigger word that had set her off?

She still had that enormous roll of banknotes in her pocket. *Her* pocket? Was it really her own money in the pocket? Somehow, she did not think so. She did not want to think at all about the brownish-red stains on some of the banknotes, but they haunted her, drifting into her mind when she least expected it.

She was sliding into a panic attack. Perhaps with good reason— that was the most panicking thought of all.

Some day, as she walked along some unfamiliar street—and they were all unfamiliar—would she feel a hand grasp her arm? Would someone make a sudden harsh demand for an accounting?

Perhaps she ought to begin to budget to replace the fifty-pound notes she had already used. When she came to a place where she could settle for a bit and work with some regularity, it might not be too difficult.

If she had that much time.

The shadows began fluttering closer again, dark and menacing. All that money, thousands and thousands. If it wasn't hers, then it must belong to someone else. Someone who would want it back.

Was someone searching for her even now?

CHAPTER 11

Time was running out. Sooner rather than later now, it was all going to blow sky high. He had to get away before that happened.

But the little bitch had run off with all his money. He had to find her first, get his money back—and finish her, before she could tell everything she knew.

Damn her! She was clever. He'd never have given her credit for being able to disappear so completely. There was no trace of her in her former haunts. She hadn't gone back to the flat. She hadn't even gone back to school. She knew what would happen to her if she did.

And she had the money. She must be spending it, she had no other way to manage. How much was she spending? And how fast?

He lay rigid staring into the pre-dawn blackness. Outside, the birds were waking up and beginning their eternal clamor. He lifted his watch and squinted at it; just before the hour. Might as well catch the news. He fumbled for his Walkman and slipped the button into his ears; the dial was permanently tuned to the news station these days. He could check every hour and on the half-hour. So far, the news he feared hadn't been discovered.

Or perhaps it hadn't been released. The police hushed things up sometimes while investigations were proceeding.

Had she gone to the police? Or had the other one?

Damn her! He'd take care of her when he found her.

Or when someone else found her. The college couldn't ignore the non-appearance of their students for much longer. Old Standfast would fight to the last ditch before notifying the police. It wouldn't look good for the school—or his record. But even he would have to do something eventually.

He wondered if Standfast might be persuaded to hire a private detective to begin making discreet inquiries. They would have to start the search some time soon.

And, when they did, he would be right there behind them.

CHAPTER 12

Dee was afraid that she should have been more forceful in her attempts to persuade Tanya to abandon the flat and move into the hotel with her. It had begun as an impulsive suggestion, and one foredoomed to failure.

As Tanya had sensibly pointed out, someone ought to remain in the flat in case Connie or one of the others telephoned. She had also pointed out that the hotel was unlikely to welcome dogs. The same arguments applied against returning to the Hall of Residence—Dee's second, and feebler, suggestion.

Tanya was right—and she was wrong. She should not be allowed to remain alone in that sinister flat, however good her reasons. Fleetingly, Dee thought of alerting the college authorities; surely they would have to do something if they knew the circumstances.

Unfortunately, she could not imagine Professor Standfast stirring himself to action for any reason at all. Dee wondered again just how good the real Dean had been. How unfortunate that he should have collapsed at this time.

She had made Tanya promise to keep in touch, that was the best she could hope for right now. She would also make it her business to check in at the flat periodically, just in case Tanya's idea of keeping in touch didn't coincide with her own. But she had noticed that Tanya had not been surprised that she had flown over here because of the silence from Connie. Also, Tanya had been uncomfortable throughout the whole interview. She thought that Tanya knew, or suspected, more than she was prepared to admit on such brief acquaintance. Another's parent was always an unknown quantity—perhaps an enemy. Winning Tanya's confidence might be a long and time-consuming struggle, but it would be necessary. Was there a way of short-circuiting the time span?

It was hopeful that—without prompting—Tanya had offered her the opportunity of looking through Connie's possessions. They hadn't revealed much except for the fact that Connie had done some enthusiastic shopping since she had been here. There were no personal papers, only schoolwork. There was also no passport, a grim reminder that Connie might not even be in the country. What could she do then? Would Continental police forces be any more helpful than the English? Somehow she doubted it.

And now she had a new worry: Tanya.

Dee tried to dismiss the memory of Tanya as she had last seen her: drawing thick curtains across the windows, blacking out the living-room completely for the few seconds it took her to reach the floorlamp and switch it on. Excusing herself, she had gone into the bedrooms and repeated the process, even though there was still some daylight outside.

Once outside herself, Dee had glanced up at the windows. Heavily shrouded by the curtains, no gleam of light showed. Anyone entering the Mews would be unaware that the flat was occupied. Was that why Tanya had chosen a silent dog, so that there would be no barking, no noise to betray her presence as she waited for the return of her flatmates?

Did Tanya really expect them to return? Dee suspected the girl had her doubts. How long would it be before she gave up hope and moved somewhere else?

Dee sighed and took the packet of Connie's letters from her handbag, sorting through them for the earliest, the ones that bore the return address of the Hall of Residence. That would be her next stop. Some of the girls who had known Connie when she lived there might have something helpful to tell her.

Princess Louise Hall was a red brick Victorian building squeezed between two modern wings of ugly concrete and glass. The little turrets, patterned stone and ironwork decorations seemed cheerful and frivolous compared to the stark determined modernity of the uncompromising wings. Dee knew which part of the building she would have preferred to live in.

The receptionist sent her into the Visitor's Lounge to wait, without confirming that either of the students she had asked for was in. Dee was studying the portrait of Princess Louise, daughter of Queen Victoria, hanging over the fireplace, when she heard footsteps hurrying down the corridor outside.

"For God's sake, Sawyer, it's about time you showed up," a voice said. "Old Marlowe is going to have your guts for garters—"

Dee turned.

"Oh! I'm sorry. I thought you were someone else."

"I'm Delia Sawyer," Dee said quietly, "Connie's mother."

"Oh shit!" The girl collapsed into the nearest chair. "It's all hitting the fan then, isn't it?"

"If you mean I've noticed that my daughter is missing, it certainly is."

"Who told you?"

"Would you believe that I was able to figure it out for myself? When I hadn't heard from Connie in three weeks, I knew something was wrong. Connie is a better correspondent than that."

"Yeah, Connie was—*is* a good kid."

"Was? Then you think something has happened to her? What do you know about it?"

"No, no, honestly, Mrs. Sawyer, that just slipped out. I don't know a thing. Not a thing!" The girl looked frightened.

"Perhaps you ought to tell me who you are," Dee said. "I asked to speak to Heidi Schnagle or Alison. I got the names from Connie's letters. Which one are you?"

"Heidi. Heidi Schnagle. From Wisconsin. I met Connie on the flight coming over. It was a good flight."

"I'm glad to hear it," Dee said drily.

"Connie's all right, I'm sure she is. Lots of kids are late getting back this term. It doesn't mean anything."

"But it isn't like Connie. Or has she changed so much in the time you've been over here? Perhaps you can tell me."

"We've all changed some," Heidi said. "We were bound to, with an experience like this. On our own in a foreign country—out in the wide world for the first time in our lives. It's a far cry from Wisconsin. And from Connecticut."

"That's what I'm afraid of," Dee said. "But you students are supposed to be supervised while you're here."

"Yeah, well," Heidi said, "there are ways around that." She seemed to remember belatedly that she was speaking to a concerned parent and added hastily, "The teachers are great, of course. They do their best but—"

"But there are ways around them."

"Well, yeah. It's not what you're thinking, though. We haven't gone wild or anything."

"Of course not," Dee said skeptically.

"Yeah, well, some of them do. But Connie didn't. And neither did I." Was there slightly too much emphasis in her defiance? But that was some other mother's problem; Dee had enough of her own.

"Look, I'm glad you came," Heidi said. "To tell the truth, I've been starting to worry and I didn't know what to do."

"It didn't occur to you to discuss it with your teachers?"

"Yeah, well, it *occurred* to me, but . . . well, I didn't want to do anything that might get Connie into trouble."

"That's presupposing she isn't in trouble already."

"Oh, I don't think so." Heidi seemed to grow paler. "Do you?"

"That's why I'm here. To find out."

"If I can help—"

"That's kind of you, Heidi, I'm going to need help." She was going to need more help than it was likely Heidi could give, but one ally was a start. If not two. Could Tanya be counted as an ally? Now that Dee thought about it, Tanya hadn't offered any active help, she had just agreed to let Dee know as soon as any of her flatmates returned.

"What about these people Connie is sharing a flat with? Can you tell me anything about them?"

"Them?" Heidi's eyes rolled wildly, seeking escape. "Oh, they're OK. Tanya is a bit strange, but maybe that's because she's English. She doesn't mix much with our group, but she's really OK, I guess."

"She seemed a little distant," Dee said, "but that might be because she's frightened."

"Frightened? What's she got to be frightened about?"

"That's what I'd like to know." Dee eyed Heidi thoughtfully; she was looking progressively more frightened herself. What were they all hiding?

"What about the others? Maggie and Jaycee?"

"Oh, they're more Tanya's friends than Connie's." Heidi seemed relieved to be able to be so definite about that point. "Jaycee is English and I think he was Tanya's boyfriend originally, before Maggie moved in on him. Maggie is a New Yorker." Her tone implied anything could be expected of *them*.

"And then they moved in together. And Tanya moved in with them? What was it, a *menage à trois*?"

"I don't think so, I think it was just finances. And, maybe, Tanya hoping she could get him back. It was Tanya, really, who persuaded Connie to share with them. You wouldn't have caught *me* moving into that horrible place. I tried to talk Connie out of it—and not just because I didn't want to lose a good room-mate. Not to mention I've got to lie like a rug to Old Mar—Miss Marlowe—and pretend Connie is still living here—" She broke off, abruptly aware of how much she was giving away.

"You mean you've been covering for Connie so that the authorities don't know she's moved?" No wonder Heidi had been so reluctant to raise the problem of Connie's disappearance with her teachers.

"Shit! I thought she'd move back here after a couple of

weeks. I never expected her to *stay* in a spooky set-up like that."

"Tanya is there alone now. Did you know that?"

"No!" Heidi shook her head emphatically. "You mean Maggie and Jaycee have moved out? I know Maggie's been bitching about finding a better place but—"

"They haven't moved out. Tanya says they went off together for the Easter holiday. They haven't come back, either."

"Oh, shit!" Heidi was alarmed now. "I don't believe this!" They looked at each other soberly. Heidi's eyes widened. "What are we going to do?" she whispered.

CHAPTER 13

Cora Trent had discovered something else about herself: she loved the sea. Something deep inside her had lightened and lifted as the bus rounded a curve and the vast expanse of water suddenly appeared in front of them.

She got off the bus, even though she had paid her fare to the end of the line. The bus might turn and head inland again and she didn't want to lose this heady feeling of lightness and joy. She couldn't bear to lose the sea, now that she had found it.

She strode along the little promenade beside the sea wall, breathing deeply. It was windy and there was a hint of impending rain in the air. The sea was dark and restless, waves rolling in, breaking on a beach that was more shale than sand. She stopped and leaned her elbows on the sea wall, savoring every moment of it.

Where the wild grey Atlantic is shouting on the shore . . .

She'd had a fairly good education, too, somewhere along the way. But she already knew that.

Live in the present! The present is all you've got! She shook herself mentally. There was no use in looking over your shoulder constantly, trying to catch a glimpse of something that wasn't there. In its own good time, maybe her mind would divulge its secrets. Or maybe it wouldn't.

Meanwhile, there was a town ahead. She began walking towards it, assessing its possibilities. She could spend tonight there, at least, although she could already see that it was too small a place to stay in for long. Also there did not seem much opportunity for casual employment. The Season was beginning, though, and there would be other, more suitable places farther along the coast. Bigger places. Cities, maybe.

She knew something else now: she wanted to settle by the sea.

Because she loved it? Or because it promised an easy and immediate escape route?

She waited, but there was no answer to that one. Just the same, when she had settled, it might not be a bad idea to make friends with a local fisherman, or some boat-owner. Just in case.

The bungalows straggling along the outskirts of the town gave way to slightly higher, more closely-packed buildings. Then the little side streets began, leading away from the promenade and up towards what was probably the High Street.

A newsagent's! Compulsively, she entered and surveyed the rack of morning papers. No headline caught her attention, but she bought a selection of them anyway. As an afterthought, she added a copy of the local weekly. She might as well begin getting an idea of what sort of jobs were likely to be available in a seaside town—and what salaries. Her best bet, though, was probably still going to be casual catering employment.

"Bed and Breakfast" signs began appearing in the windows of trim little houses. All had small front gardens, some crowded with fragrant spring flowers, some with austere pocket handkerchief lawns with a circle of more exotic vegetation centered geometrically. The less welcoming ones had had their gardens covered over with tarmac to provide a hard-standing for an automobile because there was no room for a garage.

Garage . . . Something tugged uneasily at her attention, but was gone before she could catch it, leaving that familiar sense of vague disquiet behind.

Oh no! Not on a beautiful day like this. Not when she had promised herself she was going to stop trying. Ah, but had she promised herself that to try to trick her mind into remembering? If it thought she had lost interest, it might just produce some useful information.

It didn't matter. Nothing had happened. Ignore it and it will go away. Or ignore it and it will come creeping back like a cat who doesn't really want to be bothered with you but can't stand the thought that you might not want to be bothered with it.

She walked faster, getting closer to the town center. Her attention was caught by a house just around the next corner, an end-of-terrace house with gardens on three sides and a laburnum tree in full golden shower beside a low stone wall. Instead of a fence or hedge marking the boundary on the other side, giant plumes of Pampas grass waved in the wind. A discreet sign proclaimed: Guest House.

It cost more for the room with the best sea view, but she decided to indulge herself. If she had a very late lunch, she would not need another meal, especially if she had fish and chips. That would keep her going until morning.

The room was light and airy, the furniture undistinguished but comfortable. She riffled through the daily papers, then stuffed them into the inadequate wastebasket and picked up the local paper. There would be jobs available, but it was still too small a place to stay in for long. The paper might give her a clue as to what larger cities were in the locality. If there was something within reach of the bus service, she might be able to work there for a few days and come back to this place at night . . .

It was happening again! Lately, as soon as she found a bolthole—a room—this curious reluctance to leave it overcame her. Ideally, she would like to spend a few days just living in one room, emerging only for meals and to pick up the newspapers. But she had already learned that hotels, landladies and staff did not like that; they wanted occupants out of their rooms for a goodly portion of the day, ostensibly so that the room could be serviced but actually, she suspected, because they just didn't like having people around all day.

If she found a small place of her own, a bed sitter or studio flat, she could do as she pleased in it. Yes, that was something to aim for. And she wouldn't have to register for a flat, it would just require a month's rent in advance and, possibly, a deposit. She would have to dip into the hoard of fifty-pound notes for that, but it would be in a good cause.

Someday, somehow, she would have to repay all this money she was spending. If she ever found out who it really belonged to. She hoped he didn't need the money but, judging by the cashmere coat, he probably didn't.

Perhaps . . . She tried the thought experimentally. Perhaps it was really hers. She might have earned it somehow. The mere fact that it was a man's overcoat didn't count for much of anything in these days when Unisex clothing was everywhere and the fashion was to buy what you liked from charity shops and wear it regardless.

How could she have earned that much money? That was something else she didn't like to speculate about. Not considering the obvious way a young woman could amass a large wad of fifty-pound notes. If she had been a prostitute, she had obviously been an expensive and successful one.

She found herself laughing and it felt good. How long had it been since she had laughed at anything?

No, she had never been a prostitute. Her instinctive spontaneous laughter had just told her that.

Maybe she had placed a large bet on a horse or a greyhound and won this incredible amount? That thought was funny, too.

All right, maybe she was a commercial artist and had been paid in cash for a job. Cash—as a tax dodge, so that there would be no record of any transaction and neither party would have to pay taxes—

She stopped laughing abruptly. That wasn't funny. That was . . . that was . . .

She felt the shadows swooping close to her again, swooping and enveloping her.

She just had time to throw herself down on the bed before she lost consciousness.

CHAPTER 14

Late at night, back at the hotel, Dee felt despair setting in. She was exhausted and had accomplished nothing. She was no nearer to finding Connie than she had been back in the States. She hadn't thought it would be easy, but she had thought it might be possible once she was in the same country. Now she wasn't even sure she *was* in the same country. It was difficult to realize, from three thousand miles away, just how close the mainland of Europe lay to England, how easy it was to reach.

And she had never imagined that the police could fail her. Worse, that they would be so uninterested. No wonder there were so many missing persons! How ridiculous that there should be a country where it was perfectly legal to call yourself by another name, to disappear, and where the police were reluctant to start searching until so long had passed that the trail would be cold.

Of course, if the college authorities had backed her, she might have been able to get some action. But it was only too clear that Professor Justin Standfast, Acting Dean, was not going to act. He would do nothing to jeopardize his position. It would take more than one distraught mother to make him admit that one—and possibly more—of his students had gone missing.

What would he do when he finally had to admit to himself that he had a mass disappearance on his hands? Wash his hands of it, of course. The answer came automatically. Pontius Standfast would be a better name for him.

She wouldn't let him get away with it! She'd see to it that he was called to an accounting by the Board of Trustees. And she would lodge a formal complaint with the Junior Year Abroad authorities back home. He'd pay for this dereliction of duty!

But would that help Connie?

Could anything help Connie? Or was Connie beyond help? Those were the questions lurking just below the level of her consciousness. The nightmares she was able to beat down and defeat during the day, but which crept out again with the darkness, stealing into her mind, into her dreams haunting her. She would never be free of the nightmare until she had found Connie.

If she found Connie.

What if she didn't? Other mothers had to live with this horror. Newspapers carried stories about them periodically, illustrated with pictures of haggard women with dark circles under their eyes, pathetically displaying photographs of their child as it had appeared in the last known photograph. Sometimes the photographs had been worked on by a graphic artist, "updating" them to show the way it was supposed the child might look today. Two years, five years, ten years farther on. As the artist imagined the ageing process might have gone. There was no guarantee whatsoever that the artist would be correct in his suppositions.

For some parents, the nightmare went on until the end of their lives; there was no use in pretending otherwise. They trudged the streets, moving from city to city, handing out flyers bearing the child's photograph and description, begging people to help them, clinging to the belief that their child was alive and moderately well somewhere. At night, they must be beset by horrors, too, dreaming of the mutilated body, the unmarked grave.

Sometimes the children *did* return, years later, as strangers, scarred by the experiences they had endured, barely recognizable as the ones who had gone missing. How did a parent cope with that? How did they face the accusing eyes and plead in mitigation: I tried. I tried to find you. Why didn't I succeed? Where were you? Where have you been all these years? It's been a nightmare for me, too.

Dee dried her eyes after a while and sat up straighter. It was too soon to give in to despair. Like John Paul Jones, she had not yet begun to fight.

She pulled a piece of hotel stationery towards her and, uncapping her pen, began to map out a plan of campaign. As she jotted down notes, she began to feel better, almost as though she were doing something useful. It was better than doing nothing.

For one thing, she must tackle Tanya again. Tanya was frightened and beset by her own problems, wondering when her flatmates would reappear and how long she would be left alone. Yes, and there must be the financial aspect for her to worry about, too. If the rent was too high for Maggie and Jaycee to manage together, then one student on her own would not be able to pay it. If Maggie and Jaycee had been planning to return soon after the start of term, they would not have bothered to pay their share of the rent in advance.

Had Maggie and Jaycee been planning to return? Maggie had not sounded the type to appreciate having her love-nest invaded by a couple of other females, particularly when one was an ex-rival. Heidi had said that

Maggie had been bitching about finding another place. Had Maggie succeeded in finding one? And had she and Jaycee quietly moved out, leaving Tanya to discover for herself, eventually, that she had been abandoned? Perhaps Tanya already suspected something of the sort; she must be wondering whether she would be able to get back into the Hall of Residence if she had to give up the flat. And what about the dog?

But in that case, why hadn't Maggie and Jaycee returned to their classes? Were they afraid to face Tanya after marooning her in that dreary, desolate flat?

And what about those other students who were missing? What was the explanation for them? They must have parents and friends who were beginning to worry. If all the concerned parents banded together, surely the authorities must be forced into taking action.

It did not necessarily follow—she acknowledged the weakness in her reasoning—that because a group of students were late in returning to their studies something must have happened to them all.

Professor Standfast would present a strong case against that. He had already cited the instance of the student who had taken off with a visiting relative, and the one whose parent had telephoned to report him at home with flu. Possibly others had been taken ill and, safe and cosseted in their own homes, had not thought to inform the school. When recovered, they would return to their classes with a verbal apology and that would be that.

Would it? It seemed a rather casual way to conduct an education. But everything was more casual these days. Perhaps the other students had simply decided to drop out and hadn't bothered to tell anyone. Perhaps . . .

No! Connie would never be a dropout!

She must try to discover the names of the other missing students. Somehow. Instinctively, Dee knew that Professor Standfast would be of no help to her in this. When he finally pulled his head out of the sand and looked around, would he admit that something had gone seriously wrong amid his flock?

Probably not. Probably he'd just bury his head in the sand again and hope it would all blow over. Dee wondered what the real Dean had been like. Dean Abbott *must* have had more concern for his students. Anyone must. Professor Standfast *had* to be the exception that proved the rule. What was he doing in the education field, anyway? Perhaps he had been drawn to it because he liked the long and frequent vacations. It couldn't have been because he wanted to nurture unfolding young intellects. Any young intellect that tried to flower in his vicinity was more likely to get a shot of weedkiller.

What a pity that the real Dean had had to have his stroke just at this particular time. Abruptly, the thought caught and held her. Dean Abbott had collapsed just over three weeks ago. Connie had been missing for just over three weeks. How long had the other students been missing? Was it just a coincidence? Or had something happened at the beginning of the Easter Break that had brought on the Dean's collapse?

Was there any way she could find out?

She remembered the picture on Professor Standfast's desk: the Dean's wife and family. But . . . she couldn't intrude at a time like this . . .

Why not? She hardened her heart. Did a sick man's wife deserve more consideration than the mother of a missing girl? At least the Dean's family knew where he was, that he was receiving the best medical attention, his needs monitored night and day.

If the Dean died, he would be buried decently, in a family plot, with his loved ones gathered at the graveside to weep and mourn. If Connie died . . .

Connie was alive! She had to be!

But where? Unlike the Dean, Connie might be anywhere. Or perhaps, like the Dean, she was lying in some hospital, unconscious, victim of an accident, unable to identify herself, unknown.

But when they had a case like that on their hands, a pretty young unknown girl, the hospital issued pictures to the media, asking for someone to come forward and identify her. Surely someone from the college would have recognized her and claimed her if that had happened.

Dee realized that she was trying to talk herself out of the grim task of telephoning all the London hospitals to make sure that there was no unknown girl languishing in any of them. And what of the even grimmer task of checking through the morgues? Was "Jane Doe" waiting patiently to be claimed?

London was just one city; there were so many more in this island kingdom. And just across the Channel was the whole mainland of Europe. Connie could be anywhere; she could even have gone way beyond Europe.

Dee had seen so many enticing advertisements in every travel agent's window she passed. They offered Bargain Breaks to far corners of the earth, everywhere from Nepal to Thailand to Australia or New Zealand. The prices were unbelievably low, the destinations were exotic. Connie must have been tempted a thousand times. Every time she paused before a window to read the special offers: the standby fares for those under twenty-six years of age. A student could go anywhere in the world from here, at a moment's notice. It would not be surprising if Connie had succumbed to the temptation for her Easter holiday.

But why hadn't she written? If she had gone off on a whirlwind tour, there should have been a stream of post-cards flaunting her presence in exotic locales. If only to annoy her brother. ("Yah! I got here first!") They were both guilty of the usual sibling rivalry.

Dee found that she was crying again. Angrily she brushed at the tears with the back of her hand. Crying would solve nothing; she had no time to waste on tears. She had no time—or energy—for anything else, either. Time had run out for today. It was almost midnight; she could not do anything else tonight. People had gone to bed; she ought to go to bed herself. Tomorrow was another day and she must be fighting fit—there would be a lot of fighting to do.

But there was one person she would not awaken if she telephoned now. It was seven p.m. back home, Hal should be back from the office, watching his favorite program, perhaps with a TV dinner he had heated up. And perhaps not.

She tried the number, but was not really surprised when there was no answer.

CHAPTER 15

In the morning, Dee opened the curtains to discover that it was raining. She had needed only this. Her spirits, already low, nosedived. Was this trip any use at all? Maybe Hal had been right. Maybe she was just a fool on a wild goose chase, chasing after a child who no longer wanted or needed her. Who, furthermore, would be furious when she returned in her own good time and discovered her mother had been creating a fuss.

But, if Connie was in trouble, there was no one else to help her.

Dee made a pot of tea and nibbled at a biscuit from the hospitality tray on the dressing-table. It was not really satisfactory, but she was not hungry and could not face going down to the dining-room for the Full English Breakfast. In this mood, it would probably choke her.

Before doing anything else, she made the now-ritual call to the college. The answer remained the same. No, she could not speak to Constance Sawyer. Miss Sawyer was not available right now.

So Connie had not returned overnight. Dee hadn't thought it likely. She discovered she had enough confidence in Tanya to believe that the girl would have notified her if Connie had come back to the flat last night.

And if Connie had shown up in classes, Heidi would have let her know. She began to feel better as she realized that she was not entirely without allies. It was too bad that the college authorities could not be counted among them.

Or could they? Granted, Professor Standfast was a dead loss, but there *had* been one teacher so concerned that he had telephoned Tanya because Jaycee was missing from his studies.

Dr. Carson, that was the name. *He* might listen! He might even believe that something was wrong. The fact of his telephoning seemed to indicate that, whatever his lovelife, Jaycee was not a slipshod student. And since Dr. Carson knew enough to telephone him at the flat and knew Tanya, perhaps Jaycee had confided even more to him.

Dee still had the feeling that Tanya knew a lot more than she was telling. Could Dr. Carson succeed where she herself had failed? If they both confronted Tanya, demanding more information, would they get it? Dee was increasingly sure that Tanya, like Connie in her letters home, had not actually lied, but had certainly withheld a few pertinent facts.

First, catch your Dr. Carson.

She felt a ridiculous surge of hope as she lifted the telephone. She tried to calm herself as she waited for the college switchboard to answer. It was unrealistic to pin too much faith to one person. The past few days had taught her that she was in for a long haul, battling uphill all the way.

"Good morning. May I speak to Dr. Carson, please?" She held her breath waiting for the response. At this point, she would not be surprised to find that he, too, had quietly joined the missing.

"One moment, please." They were putting her through.

She tightened her grip on the receiver, still prepared for disappointment.

"Carson here." The voice was crisp and authoritative, inspiring instant confidence. This sounded like a man who knew what he was doing—unlike Professor Standfast.

"Dr. Carson, I'd like to talk to you—"

"Speaking!" There was a trace of irritation in his tone. Dee realized that she had been so intent on contact that she had skipped the necessary preliminaries.

"Dr. Carson, I'm sorry. This is Delia Sawyer speaking. I'm Constance Sawyer's mother. I was in the flat yesterday when you rang about Jaycee and talked to Tanya—"

"The flat?"

"The flat they're all sharing in Coram's Mews. My daughter—"

"Mrs. Sawyer, I'd like to see you. We have matters to discuss."

"That's what I was thinking."

"I have a lecture in ten minutes. You just caught me before I left the office. I'll be through by eleven. Shall we say eleven-thirty?" He took her agreement for granted. "Not here, I think. Do you know the Museum Tavern? It's the pub on the corner of Museum Street and Great Russell Street."

"I'll find it," she said.

"It's hard to miss." There was a trace of amusement in his voice. "It's right opposite the British Museum. I'll see you there."

He was gone before Dee could ask how she was to recognize him. Presumably he anticipated no difficulty in picking her out of the crowd. He must have dealt with anxious mothers before.

The dark grey bulk of the British Museum was imposing, yet not forbidding, set well back behind iron railings on one side of a tree-lined street. Small shops and publishers lined the street as Dee approached from Tottenham Court Road, giving it a friendly and accessible ambience. It was one of the places Dee had planned to explore—with Connie.

The pub was on a corner opposite the gates. Hanging baskets of flowers, engraved frosted glass windows and trimmings of shiny brass gave it a welcoming appearance. Still Dee hesitated. She had never gone into a pub before. She scanned the faces of approaching pedestrians hopefully, but she had formed no mental picture of Dr. Carson and she could not accost complete strangers on the off chance that one of them might be the man she was meeting. She would have to go in alone.

The pub was beginning to fill up. It appeared to be a favorite luncheon place for students and research workers using the British Museum. Dee bagged a table while there was still one available. Having got it, she did not dare leave it, not even to go up to the bar. She didn't want a drink, anyway. It was much too early—although no one else in the place seemed to feel so. She hoped she did not look as out-of-place as she felt.

"Mrs. Sawyer?" He had found her.

"Dr. Carson?" She looked up, then lowered her sights. He was shorter than she had expected. The voice had led her to expect someone of Hal's size—over six feet. Dr. Carson was about five feet six, and chunky with it. His shoulders were broad and powerful. Dark-eyed and dark-haired, he gave off an impression of bull-like strength and energy.

"I'll get us a drink. What are you having?"

"I don't—"

"Don't say you don't drink. Or you're on one of those Perrier water kicks. I've no time for quirky women."

"I don't usually drink this early," Dee said indignantly. "It's still morning."

"Only just. You don't know what you want, do you?"

I want my daughter . . . but it was too soon to start on that problem. Not with him hovering over her impatiently; obviously she was keeping him from his own drink.

"Beer? Do you like English beer? Or gin and tonic?"

"I don't like any beer. And I don't want gin at this hour." How had she got trapped in this ridiculous dialogue when there was such an important issue at stake?

"We'll try you on cider, then," he decided, to his own satisfaction, if not to hers. "Back in a minute."

She watched him thrust his way through the crowd, unerringly winding up at the one spot where a barmaid was just about to wait on another customer. He deflected her attention without effort. He said a few words to the people around him and everybody laughed. No one seemed to mind that he had pushed in front of them.

"Now then—" He placed a beaker of amber liquid in front of her and set down his own foaming mug without spilling a drop. "Wrap your tonsils around that. And then we'll talk."

"I'm ready to talk now." Dee lifted her glass but did not sip from it.

"Well, I'm not." He gulped a long draught. "It's thirsty work, trying to ram some knowledge into heads of solid bone."

Dee felt a wave of annoyance wash over her. Did no one in this country have any respect for their students? She tried to imagine an American teacher making a remark like that to a parent. It would set the Parent-Teacher Association ablaze with demands for apologies—if not resignations.

"That's better." Sublimely unaware of his imagined fate at the hands of incensed American organizations, Dr. Carson set his glass down on the table and leaned towards Dee. "Now, what's this all about?"

"I was hoping you might be able to tell me." As she watched his eyebrow quirk upwards, she realized how frail that hope was. Why should he keep track of his students in their off-time? He obviously didn't care much about them when they were in his lecture room.

"I'm sorry. I shouldn't have bothered you." She began to stand up, then remembered. "But there's no one else. I thought you might be able to help—"

"Sit down." His hand closed over her wrist; he studied her for a moment. "When did you last eat?"

"I—I don't remember. It's not important—"

"It is if you expect to make any sense. Stay here. I'll be right back."

She leaned back and closed her eyes, trying to gather herself together. He was right: she was making no sense. And it was so important, so desperately important—for Connie's sake—that she did.

"Here . . . " He returned before she had halfway formulated the arguments she intended to use. There was the clink of a plate being set down on the tabletop, followed by the clatter of cutlery escaping from a tightly-furled paper napkin.

"Oh." She opened her eyes and looked at the laden plate in front of her. "Cottage pie."

"Shepherd's pie," he corrected. "No matter. Mince and

mashed potatoes—always safe. Eat and drink up, then we'll talk."

He had brought two long fat sausages for himself, beside them a mountain of mashed potato rose out of a sea of gravy surrounding an island of green peas. Obviously not a man to be intimidated by cholesterol. Perhaps he wouldn't be intimidated by other problems, either.

The pie was delicious, hot and savory. How long *had* it been since she had eaten? To her embarrassment, she finished the heaping plateful well ahead of her host.

"Good!" He nodded approval. "Want a refill?"

"Heavens, no! I couldn't!" It was probably the truth, but she hoped he wouldn't put it to the test.

"More cider, anyway." He pushed back his chair and was at the bar before she could protest. Again he worked his dubious magic on everyone in front of him, returning with fresh drinks for both of them.

"All right." He gave her a sharp glance before turning his attention back to his remaining sausage. "Suppose you tell me what this is all about."

"My daughter—Connie—" She had to plunge straight in, there was no easy lead-up. "My daughter is missing."

"Ah." He seemed neither surprised nor concerned. "And what do you think I can do about it?"

"I don't know. But you're a teacher—"

"She wasn't in any of my classes." The denial was quick. Too quick?

"Perhaps not, but Jaycee was. I know you're concerned about him—I was at the flat when you telephoned and talked to Tanya. I thought—"

"You think they've eloped?"

"No!" She had never considered that. "Of course not! He was living with Maggie."

"Little devils! I might have known it." He was midway between annoyance and amusement. "You can't take your eyes off them for one minute." Amusement won; he snorted with laughter. "No wonder his work was deteriorating."

"I'm glad you think it's funny," she said coldly. "Maggie is missing, too."

"'Missing' is an emotive word." He looked at her thoughtfully. "Are you quite sure there isn't a simpler explanation?"

"You sound like Professor Standfast." She could not keep the bitterness out of her voice. "He doesn't want to believe it, either."

"He wouldn't," Dr. Carson agreed. "Anything for a quiet life, that's our Justin."

"It won't be quiet if I don't find my daughter!" Her voice was growing shriller. She took a deep breath and tried to bring it under control. It would do no good to alienate this man. "I suppose you think it's silly of me to worry like this?"

"On the contrary, I think it's extremely sensible of you. Most of us teachers spend a great deal of time worrying—and we have a better idea of what there is to worry about."

"What?" His sudden agreement disconcerted her.

"Drugs, for a start, that's the most obvious problem. We keep a watch for the telltale signs. But you wouldn't believe what else the little darlings can get up to. They're away from home—some of them for the first time in their lives—living in a big sophisticated city. They want to be part of it; they think just living here makes them sophisticated, too. All those silly things the family warned them about—forget them. They're too smart for their breeches!

The White Slave Trade still exists—but do you think we can convince them of that?"

"White Slave Trade," Dee echoed faintly. She realized that she was someone else who had thought it could not exist in this day and age. Her *grandmother* had been given to dire warnings about that, for heaven's sake. In her worst imaginings, she had never thought of that. She had also tried not to think about pornography rackets and serial killers.

"There's a brisk market in certain Third World countries for young white girls—and boys, too. And they needn't think they're safe just because they don't intend to answer any advertisements to go and be cabaret dancers in Marrakesh. A few chance encounters with their friendly local pimp will serve to target them—"

"That's incredible!" She was still fighting against the horrible pictures crowding into her mind. Connie—in a situation like that!

"It may be incredible in Smalltown, USA," he said grimly. "It's one of the Facts of Life here."

"Smalltown, USA, isn't immune any more!" Dee flared. "Children go missing all too often. But we try harder to find them. Their pictures are printed on milk cartons, shopping-bags, posted in public places . . . " She faltered, seeing in her mind's eye the blurred, pathetic photos. "If Connie was a child, the police would be looking for her now. Even here—"

"That's another part of the problem," he said. "The police have to be so careful in dealing with adults. There's always the chance that she's moved in with a boyfriend. The other girls in the Residence think it's very romantic, you know, and they'll cover for the girls who move out to live with boyfriends. That's something else we have to be on the lookout for." He paused. "You're sure . . . ?"

"No, she moved out—but not because of that. It was to help her friends pay the rent on the flat—" Or had Heidi been lying to her about that? How much rent could a landlord demand for a ratty, miserable flat like that?

"I'm not sure of anything any more." She fought back tears. "There are so many terrible possibilities—"

"Yes." He seemed determined to spare her nothing. "Sex murders happen, as well. Probably more frequently than we realize, since it can take months or years before the bodies are discovered. If they ever are. Until that time, they're listed as missing persons."

"You're being a great comfort to me." She started fighting back. "I'm so glad I called on you for help!"

"Refusing to face the facts won't change them." He slanted an oblique look at her. "I thought you wanted me to take you seriously but, when I do, you complain."

"I'm sorry. You're right." Had he been testing her, trying to decide if she was a complete idiot? "I've thought of that, of course. I've been living with it for weeks. It's just that—" Her voice wavered, she took a deep breath and continued. "It's just a shock to hear it put into words. By someone else."

"That's better." He nodded approval; she had passed the test. "Naturally it's a shock. It's been a shock to me, too. I hadn't thought anything worse than that young Jaycee was dragging his heels about resuming his studies. It never occurred to me that he had gone missing. I'm afraid I barely know your daughter; she isn't in any of my classes. I have a vague idea I might know her by sight—if she bears any resemblance to you."

"We've been mistaken for sisters." She flushed, that was an idiotic thing to say. This was no time for vanity.

"Then I've seen her around. Usually with a couple of friends. Not all American, I think. She seemed to be doing better than most at broadening her acquaintance."

"She would," Dee said proudly. "She was so excited about coming over here. She wanted to meet everyone, see everything, *do* everything——" Her treacherous voice betrayed her again.

"Right." He became excessively businesslike, ignoring the fact that she was groping for a handkerchief. "Then we'd better map out some sort of plan of action. As soon as—I mean *if*—we get anything to go on, we can take it to the police and let them take over."

"Yes." She used the handkerchief briefly, then whisked it out of sight again, cheered by the prospect of action. "Well, I thought *you* might talk to Professor Standfast. He said there were about six students who hadn't returned to classes yet, but he didn't tell me who they were. I know about Maggie, Jaycee . . . and Connie. You might be able to get the other names."

"Good point," he said. "I probably could. In fact, there'd be no need to talk to Standfast at all, I can go round him and get it from the attendance records. If Standfast thinks there's trouble brewing, he won't be anxious to speak to me, either."

"Then we can check with their families and friends," she said, refusing to be diverted by Professor Standfast's peculiarities. "Someone might know what plans they had for their holiday. They might even know where they are and why they haven't come back."

"*If* they're all together." He sounded a note of caution. "But, yes, it opens out more possibilities. They might have booked a holiday with some dodgy travel agent who's gone bust and left them stranded on some island in the Indian Ocean or somewhere where communication isn't too easy."

"I hadn't thought of that." Hope flared, strengthening her.

"It happens. A few agencies go down every season. But," he added carefully, "don't count on that as the explanation. It's more probable that they've all gone off independently and it will turn out that one or two are nursing broken bones after falls while rock-climbing and the others have succumbed to flu."

"One of them phoned in to say he had flu," she remembered. "But Professor Standfast didn't tell me which one."

"He wouldn't," Dr. Carson said. "Don't worry, we'll find out."

CHAPTER 16

She *wasn't* afraid of the dark! She couldn't be! That was for children. She was a grown-up, a young woman.

She couldn't deny, however, that her spirits sank with the sinking sun, When the grey gloom of twilight darkened into blackness, so did her mood. Problems that had seemed relatively minor in the light of day now looked impossible to solve. Fears she had learned to suppress now fought their way free and stalked her afresh. Yes, and the deeper shadows had begun to flutter at the edge of her consciousness and were preparing to swoop again.

She stretched out her hand and snapped on the bedside lamp.

The unfamiliar room instantly gave up all its secrets. Sparsely furnished (well, at the price she was paying, she was lucky to have any furniture at all), drably painted, dull and dreary though it was, it was home for the foreseeable future.

She hated falling asleep in the middle of the afternoon. It meant you woke at the worst possible time, daylight gone, but too early in the evening to be able to turn over and go to sleep again and sleep the night through. She was nagged by the guilty feeling that she had lost the best part of the day—but what would she have done with it if she'd been awake? The hollow emptiness dragged at her, depressing her, making her wonder if it was worth going on . . .

And that was enough of that! She bounded out of bed and stood blinking in the middle of the room. There were enough damned questions on the practical aspects of life alone—never mind bringing metaphysics into it!

Net curtains fluttered at the open window and she crossed the room to slam the window shut and draw the drapes. It was too cold for an open window once the sun went down. No wonder she felt a chill.

But it was sea air that had been blowing through the room and her spirits began to rise. The sea meant safety. She caught the thought and tried to analyze it. Why the sea? It wasn't just any old stretch of water, she was sure. She could think of ponds and lakes without any instinctive surge of warmth and security. Rivers were downright hostile, treacherous and deadly . . .

She shivered again. Not just from the chill this time. Her mind winced away from a pathway it did not wish to explore. Don't force it . . . don't force it . . .

She took a few deep breaths and the darkness within her mind receded. She took another deep breath and her stomach rumbled. She caught back a laugh. Nature had such inelegant ways of reminding one of one's mortality.

But, now that it had been brought to her attention, she was hungry. Very hungry. It was time she did something about it.

She would have to go out into the dark night.

Her mind protested, her stomach growled again.

It wasn't *so* dark, she reasoned with herself. The sky was pink with the glow reflected from one of the biggest cities along the coast. There were plenty of streetlights along the way. Once in the city, she would find lights, people, laughter—most important, restaurants and eating houses. She had already decided to eat every meal in a different place until she found one that was congenial, busy—and in need of more staff.

But, the newly-discovered fear tugged at her, if she got a job in a restaurant, she would have to be out late at night every night. She would always be coming back to her lodgings in the darkness.

She *wasn't* afraid of the dark! She had already established that with herself. She might prefer not to be out in it, but she wasn't actually afraid of it. Not really.

Besides, there was nothing else she could do right now. She needed money; she couldn't go on using the bankroll she had found in her possession. For her own self-respect and peace of mind, she needed money she had earned herself. For the moment, working in catering was the fastest and easiest way to earn it.

Later, as she grew more self-assured—and learned more about what she could and could not do—she might be able to find a job doing something else. She had a vague feeling that she might be able to type, but she wanted to test it out before she presented herself for an office job. There was also the danger that she might be asked too many questions if she applied for a permanent job. But that was something that would have to be faced in the future.

Right now, the future would have to take care of itself. Even the problem of the dark would soon be solved—for the summer, at least. It was spring already and, in a couple of weeks, the clocks would be turned ahead an hour. And the days were lengthening naturally, too. It wouldn't be so bad.

A tall narrow wardrobe leaned against the wall next to the door. She opened it and looked with dissatisfaction at the few items she possessed, hanging like lost souls in a vast cavern. She was going to need more to wear. She grinned wryly. Already she hated every rag she owned. And the paucity of her luggage had been the cause of some comment on the part of her landlady.

"Hmm," the woman had said, looking thoughtfully at her small holdall. "DHSS, are you?"

"Oh no," Connie had replied quickly, somehow knowing that the initials referred to being on the dole. "No, I'm a student."

"Oh yes." The woman's face cleared. "With that accent, you would be, wouldn't you? Going to one of the language schools for some cramming, are you?"

"That's right." It was easy to talk to the woman since she obligingly supplied the answers to her own questions. But the reference to an accent was disconcerting.

"American, are you?" the woman persisted. "Or Canadian?"

"Canadian." Cora wasn't sure, but something told her that it would be wiser to opt for a country still connected to Britain, however loosely. For one thing, it would make it easier to get a job.

"Well, I'll show you the room . . . " The woman still seemed a bit reluctant. "Of course, it might not be good enough for you. Not the sort of thing you're used to . . . "

Cora smiled and shrugged. She didn't know what she was used to. "I'm supposed to be studying," she answered in line with the role to which she had been assigned.

"Here we are." It had been the right answer; the woman smiled as she turned the knob and flung open the door.

"This is fine," Cora said. "Just fine." For the first time, she felt genuine enthusiasm as she looked around. Never mind that the few bits of furniture were shabby and the paint was dingy, there was a tiny Baby Belling electric hob and oven in one corner. Even better, the other corner had been squared off to house a shower stall, toilet and sink. It was self-contained: she would not have to share a kitchen and bathroom and risk meeting other tenants.

"I have a cheaper room—" The bargaining began. "But it's not so big and you'd have to share the bathroom on the landing. You might not like that."

"No, this will do." She had taken the precaution of removing two fifty-pound notes from the bankroll and tucking them into the cheap shoulder-bag she had bought. The avid flash of the woman's eyes as she opened her bag made her realize how wise this had been.

"I'll need a deposit, of course," the woman said. "And students usually have a six- or eight-week rental. But you're late, the term has already started—Are you all right?"

"Yes . . ." Sudden dizziness had caught her, weakening her knees and forcing her to slump down on the edge of the bed.

"You're not sick, are you?" The woman's voice sharpened with suspicion. "Or pregnant?"

"Of course not!" The denial was so indignant, so automatic, that she surprised even herself.

"Well, I'm sorry." The woman was abashed. "But you don't know what I have to put up with. The tricks some of them try—"

"I'm sorry, I didn't mean to snap at you." Cora apologized in turn, not because she was contrite, but because she was afraid of antagonizing the woman. This room was looking better to her by the minute. She didn't want to risk losing it.

"I'm just—" She had a flash of inspiration— "I'm just jet-lagged. And I didn't eat much on the plane. The food was so— ''

"Oh yes, it's frightful, isn't it?" Eager to make amends, the landlady rushed to agree. "Plastic, just plastic. No taste at all. I never eat it myself."

Cora nodded weakly. "And I'm so tired," she said, half to herself.

"Why don't I get you a nice cup of tea?" The landlady was all concern now. "And perhaps some toast? Then you can lie down and have a little rest before you go back and get the rest of your luggage."

"I'm so tired," Cora said cautiously, "I might let that wait until tomorrow." She'd be able to buy something passable when the stores were open. "But some tea sounds wonderful." She smiled wanly. "If I can stay awake long enough to drink it."

The cup, half full of cold unappealing liquid, stood on the bedside table now. Tactfully, Cora emptied it down the sink. If Mrs. Lane chose to investigate her room in her absence, she didn't want to leave proof that the offering was unappreciated. For a moment, she considered carrying the empty dishes down into the kitchen, but that would lead to a conversation. And that would be too much to handle. She knew that her powers of invention were flagging as surely as her energy at this hour. It would be best just to slip out quietly and find some place to eat. With luck, she might also get back into the house and regain her room unobserved.

Concentrating on leaving her room silently and getting down the stairs unseen helped her to avoid thinking about the faint sensation of panic bubbling just below the level of her consciousness. As the front door closed behind her, she swallowed hard and stepped out into the darkness. She forced herself to walk down the path briskly, not giving way to the panic attack. There was nothing to be afraid of here.

Was there?

CHAPTER 17

When Dee got back to the hotel, Heidi was waiting in the lobby, slumped in a big wing chair, a book open on her lap and a large suitcase at her feet. A suitcase Dee recognized immediately—she had helped to pack it just a few months ago.

"Heidi! That's Connie's case! Is she back?"

"Oh shit! You made me jump!" Heidi bent double to retrieve the book that had slipped from her lap. "I didn't hear you come up behind me. Of course, this carpet is so thick—"

"It *is* Connie's case!" She hadn't meant to sound accusing, but Heidi flinched. "Her nametag is still on the handle. Where is she?" Dee looked around wildly, half-expecting Connie to rush into her arms, laughing.

"Hey, take it easy, Mrs. Sawyer!" Heidi stretched out a hand nervously, not quite daring to touch her. "I'm sorry. Connie isn't back. Sure, it's her suitcase. She never took it with her. It—it's been in our room all along. I just forgot about it."

"You forgot!" Dee glared at Heidi, no longer worried about seeming censorious. "How could you forget a thing like that?"

"Well, OK. I mean, I just didn't think it was important. Connie said she was just leaving a few things she didn't feel like moving over to the flat. Things she never used very much. And, I think, she wanted to keep some things around so that she could stay overnight in the Hall if she wanted to. Toothbrush and pajamas— things like that. But after I talked to you, I got to thinking. Maybe there's something in it she might not have wanted to leave lying around the flat where anybody could see it. A diary, maybe, or something like that."

"And is there?"

"How would I know?" Heidi was aggrieved. "I don't go around breaking open locked suitcases. But I thought maybe you could. I mean, Connie couldn't complain if you broke the lock."

"Come upstairs." Dee picked up the suitcase as Heidi made a feebly helpful snatch at it. Now that she had it, it was going to stay in her possession. Heidi followed her to the elevator and shifted from foot to foot uneasily as they waited for it to arrive.

Lost in thought, Dee did not speak again until she had closed the door of her room behind them. This seemed to make Heidi uneasier than ever. She shied back involuntarily when Dee set the suitcase down with a thump and turned to her.

"Now," Dee said. "Let's get a few things straight."

"Sure, Mrs. Sawyer. Sure." Placating wasn't the word for it, Heidi was close to grovelling. The girl obviously had something on her conscience. There were no prizes for guessing what it was.

"All right." Dee held out her hand, palm upwards. "Let's have the key."

"The key?" Heidi shied back still farther. In another moment she would be against the wall.

"The key," Dee said firmly. "Do you really expect me to believe that you don't have it? That you haven't opened the case?"

"Oh shit! Look, Mrs. Sawyer, I can explain—"

"Later." Dee waggled her fingers. "First, give me the key."

With a sigh of resignation, Heidi delved into one of the many little pockets secreted about her jacket and pulled out the miniature key. "I don't see how you knew," she complained, handing it over. "You're worse than *my* mother. I could never get away with anything with her, either."

Dee took the key and concentrated on dealing with the tiny padlock. If Heidi chose to believe that adults possessed some superior antennae, it was obviously wiser not to disillusion her. It might be necessary to bluff through on that assumption on some future occasion. This was just the beginning, not the end, of their association.

"And there *is* a diary." Dee flipped back the lid and was not surprised to see the slim volume lying on top of the clothing.

"Give me *some* credit," Heidi pleaded. "I thought first I'd mail it to you anonymously. But that would have taken an extra day—more if it got held up in the post. And besides, the names and initials wouldn't mean anything to you. I knew you'd need someone to interpret it for you."

"And you've already read it." Dee was able to interpret the last few remarks without difficulty.

"I thought—I hoped—I might find something to tell me where she was. Then I could contact her and bring her back myself. Without bothering you."

"I see." Dee also saw that reading it had given Heidi the opportunity to check whether anything detrimental had been written about her or any mutual friends, a chance to censor the diary before she passed it on. Dee riffled through the pages quickly; there didn't seem to be any missing.

"I didn't have to do this, you know." Heidi was offended. "I could have just thrown the thing away. Or forgotten about the suitcase entirely. You couldn't have gone through my room without a search warrant."

"I'm sorry, Heidi." Dee doubted Heidi's grasp of legalities, but was aware of her burgeoning hostility. She must not keep putting the girl on the defensive. Heidi was trying to be helpful.

"You're right." She smiled at Heidi and watched the girl begin to relax. "I'm being unfair. I really *am* grateful to you for bringing this to me. Why don't you sit down while I glance through it. Would you like some tea? I'll ring Room Service—"

"You'll be lucky!" Heidi's good humor was restored. "Why do you think you've got an electric kettle and everything on the service tray? That's English Hotelese for 'Don't bother us. Make your own tea.' Look, why don't I make the tea while you start reading?"

When Heidi set the cup on the small table beside her Dee closed the diary with a sigh. "So many names, fleeting impressions, plans—" Her voice broke momentarily. "At least she was having a good time."

"Hey, Mrs. Sawyer!" Heidi was alarmed. "Don't say it like that. Sure, she was having a great time. The time of her life—I mean, probably she still is. Somewhere. She may be having such a wonderful time that she's forgotten all about school—"

"You sound like my husband," Dee said bitterly. "You should meet him. You'd get on well with him. Too bad he's already been taken. Away from me, I mean—"

"Mrs. Sawyer!" The sudden rush of raw adult emotion was too much for Heidi to cope with. "Take it easy, Mrs. Sawyer. Drink your tea. You'll feel better."

Would she? With a wry grimace, Dee lifted her cup and took a sip. There was too much sugar in it. Because Heidi was so young and still had a sweet tooth? Or because Heidi knew that hot sweet tea was recommended for someone in a state of shock?

"Have a cookie? I mean, biscuit?" Heidi tore at the wrapper of a small packet. "They're not bad." She thrust a crumbling biscuit into Dee's hand.

"That's better." Heidi brought her own cup of tea over and perched on the end of the bed, surveying Dee like an anxious probationary nurse. "Go on, drink up."

Dee obediently took another swallow and managed not to choke on the unaccustomed sweetness.

"And eat your biscuit," Heidi cajoled.

Dee nibbled at it, sending a shower of crumbs down into her lap. They spilled across the diary and she snatched it up, shaking them off violently. It was all she had left of Connie; while she was reading it, she could hear Connie's voice bubbling in her ear.

"Let me take it." Heidi reached out for the diary. "Please? I want to show you something."

Reluctantly, Dee allowed Heidi to take the diary from her hand. She watched as Heidi flipped the pages to a point just a few pages before the last entry.

"It's this bit here," Heidi said, frowning. "It doesn't make sense. It's some kind of note to herself. Do you think it's one of her private jokes?"

Dee took the diary and looked at the cryptic entry Heidi had indicated. It was just a few words and she read it several times.

"MASS OBBO—*why not me?*"

It meant nothing to her, either.

"Do you think maybe she didn't know how to spell oboe?" Heidi asked hopefully.

"Would it make sense to you, if that were so?"

"Not quite," Heidi admitted regretfully. "But it could be a starting point. I mean, we could ask around to find out if she knew any oboe-players and was planning to take lessons."

"Connie was never very musical," Dee said doubtfully. "Do you know any musicians at all?"

"Well, no, but somebody might have a hidden talent we haven't found out about yet." Heidi paused, considering the idea, and shook her head. "Do you think it might make more sense if we weren't American?" she asked. "Maybe to an English person?"

"That's a possibility." Dee immediately thought of Tanya. "Maybe we could ask one."

"Or else there's the Mass bit. The only Masses I know are the religious kind, or the state. But you're from Connecticut, aren't you?"

"Yes." Dee stared at the scrawled words.

"Well, did she ever write anything to you about getting religion? Not that I see where she could have gotten it around these parts. They don't go in for it much over here. And there haven't been any revival meetings that I've heard of."

"No," Dee said thoughtfully. "That doesn't sound like Connie, either. There must be some other explanation." It might be, as Heidi had suggested, some private joke which had nothing to do with Connie's plans—or her disappearance.

"There's something else—" Heidi glanced uneasily towards the suitcase. "I thought you'd unpack the whole thing and see it, but you stopped at the diary—"

"What?" Dee dived for the suitcase and began pulling out the few garments—just Connie's nightclothes, spare make-up kit, a couple of sweaters and a skirt. It was folded up in the maroon lambswool cardigan. It dropped to the bed.

"Oh God!" Dee stared down at it in dismay. "It's her passport!"

"At least that means she's still in this country." Heidi

tried to be cheerful. "I mean, she isn't moldering in some French or Spanish jail . . . or . . . or something."

Or murdered in a European ditch. Dee filled in Heidi's delicate hesitations. Connie, lying in some corner of a foreign field that would be for ever Connecticut—until someone discovered the body and they could ship her home for burial.

Dee drew a quivering breath. It sounded suspiciously like a sob.

"Hey, look!" Heidi tried to encourage her. "That's *good* news. It means we don't have to worry about all the rest of the world. She's still here in England—well, the United Kingdom—somewhere. That narrows the field a lot."

"It still leaves a lot of ground to cover." Dee tried to respond to Heidi's optimism, but her tone was doleful.

"Yeah, but at least we've got a sort of a map." Heidi picked up the diary. "There's *got* to be some kind of clue in here—if we can just figure out what it is."

"*If* . . . "

"Let's start at the beginning, the first entry—"

The telephone startled them both. Dee stared at it blankly for a moment. Who could be calling her here?

"Aren't you going to answer it?" Heidi stared at her. "It has to be for you. Nobody knows I'm here."

"I—Yes—" Dee hurried to the phone, afraid that it might stop ringing before she reached it. She knew who it must be. "Hal—?"

"Hello? Mrs. Sawyer? Hello? Carson here."

"Oh, hello, Dr. Carson," she said slowly. She had forgotten about him. Why couldn't it have been Hal? (Because he doesn't care enough to call.) Where was Hal and what was he doing? (Do you need to ask?)

"I have those names," Carson reported. "Do you still want them?"

"Oh yes! Yes, please, Dr. Carson. The sooner the better." She felt a surge of hope. Something was happening, after all. And she was not completely alone. She smiled at Heidi, who was listening with interest.

"I thought so." There was a note of caution in his voice. "Perhaps you wouldn't mind telling me precisely what you intend to do with them?"

"I intend to contact their families—" She had already told him this. "Immediately. I want to find out if any of the families knew where they were going, who they were going with—and when they planned to return."

"That's rather what I understood." Dr. Carson's voice sounded odd. "I think we'd better have a drink and discuss this."

"We've just *had* a drink," Dee protested.

"That was lunch-time," he answered firmly. "You're allowed another after six o'clock. I suggest we meet at the Fair Young Maiden, it's along the Embankment near Charing Cross—" He gave brief directions and added firmly, brooking no argument, "I'll meet you there at seven."

He had rung off before she could say anything else.

CHAPTER 18

Before Heidi left, they had gathered a list of names and initials, only a few of which Heidi was unable—or unwilling—to identify. Some of these were already familiar to Dee, they included Connie's flatmates and teachers, as well as other students and friends. It would be interesting to see if any of these names tallied with those on the list of missing students to be provided by Dr. Carson.

However, there was still nearly two hours before she was due to meet Dr. Carson and she was too restless to do nothing. Time enough, Dee decided, to pay another visit to the flat in Coram's Mews. Tanya might have had some news, or might have remembered something that would help in the search.

After Heidi left, Dee put Connie's passport and diary into an envelope, sealed the envelope and wrote her name and the date across the flap. Then she stopped at the reception desk downstairs and had the envelope put into the hotel safe. It was a sensible thing to do, she told herself, avoiding the thought that the documents might be needed later . . . for evidence.

Curious glances made her aware that she was almost running as she crossed the lobby and pushed the front door open with such force that it struck against the glass wall. With a conscious effort, she slowed her steps, still moving rapidly, but without that hint of panic, as she headed for Coram's Mews. The panic was still there, buried so deep inside her that she might never be free of it again, but there was no need to advertise it to onlookers. Panic was too close to hysteria—and people hesitated to get involved with a hysterical woman. She had to be under control before she faced Tanya again, before she talked to Dr. Carson.

Hal had always accused her of being hysterical any time she tried to talk to him about any subject he wished to avoid. Lately there hadn't been many subjects they could discuss. And somehow or other, it had all been her fault.

It had even been her fault that Connie had not been content to remain in her own American college until graduation. Hal had admitted no sense of adventure, no soaring excitement of youth, no dreams of glory or exploration in a foreign setting. No. If her mother had brought her up properly, Connie would never have raised her eyes above the limited horizon of small town life and dreamed of an outside world in which she might play a greater part. It was all Dee's fault.

Strange that it had taken her so many years to realize that nothing had ever been Hal's fault. Hal had been responsible for the major decisions in life: where to live, what firm to devote his energies to, what investments to make, what schools his children should attend (until Connie grew old enough to rebel), what lifestyle best suited his needs . . .

Which woman he wished to spend the remainder of his life with . . . He had stopped worrying about Connie then. About anyone. Good old Hal, everybody's pal. Except for the wife he had vowed to love, honor and cherish until death did them part. Except for the family he had decided he had outgrown; since he no longer needed them, it must follow that they no longer needed him. Off with the old, on with the new . . .

Dee paused at the corner, her vision blurred. She hadn't been this upset when she was at home, right in the middle of the situation, so why should it bother her so much now? Was it that distance, rather than lending enchantment, was providing a clearer view? Again she tried to call herself to order. This would do no good at all. The past was past.

At least—she struggled to hold on to the reality of what had happened—what was happening—trying to sort out what was genuinely past from the past that had been imposed on her. Her husband was deliberately, and of his own free will, in the process of walking away from the life they had shared, choosing to turn to a new, younger, woman and the benefits he believed that woman could offer him.

But Connie . . . had Connie been offered a choice at all? It was all very well for Hal to pontificate now about young (and even older) people wanting their own lives, but Connie had been happy with the life she had had. Connie had not been straining at the leash towards some mythical concept called "Freedom'—that had been Hal imposing his own interpretation, colored by his own view of the life-choice he believed it was time for him to make.

Connie had had as much freedom as she needed—and wanted—at this stage of her development. Connie would *not* have chosen to disappear voluntarily—that was Hal's dream, imposed upon her. Connie had no need to remove herself from a life she was enjoying and a future she was eagerly anticipating.

Therefore . . . Dee's thoughts faltered, her footsteps quickened again. Therefore . . . Connie had *not* gone missing of her own accord. Whatever had happened to her had not been voluntary . . . had not been cold-bloodedly planned.

Connie was in some kind of trouble; trouble not of her own making. Dee's vision blurred again and she fumbled in her pocket for a paper handkerchief. Grief, to the uninitiated, was indistinguishable from hysteria; she had to be careful.

She came upon the turning so suddenly that she almost

missed it. Once again, the mews appeared desolate and abandoned, unwelcoming. Daylight was beginning to fade, although it would be another hour or so before it was completely dark, but she saw that the curtains in the flat had already been closed against the encroaching night.

Instinctively, Dee kept close to the buildings on the shadowed side of the mews. There was no reason why she should not have walked down the middle of the rough, cobbled, narrow way, except that something about the atmosphere encouraged stealth.

There was no suggestion of sidewalk; there wouldn't be, of course. As Connie had explained in her diary, mews were meant to be stable-facilities for the carriages and horses of the well-to-do in the nearby town houses. After dropping off the gentry at their front doors, the coachman had driven round to the mews running parallel with the street of town houses and stabled the horses and carriage before climbing the stairs to his own quarters above the stables.

"I'm starting out in a mews," Connie had written with bubbling excitement, *"but what do you want to bet that I'll wind up in one of those fancy town houses before I'm done?"*

Before I'm done . . . Connie . . .

Tears blinded Dee's eyes and she did not see the small patch of grease on which she slipped. She flung out her hand to save herself and gave it a nasty crack against the dusty window of the garage.

Catching her breath at the sudden pain, Dee leaned against the garage door, rubbing her hand gently, waiting for the pain to subside, half-afraid she might have broken the window.

Perhaps the garage wasn't abandoned after all, she

thought vaguely, looking down at her feet. That was fresh grease, thick and slippery, the mark of a careless workman, or of repairs done in a hurry.

Dee turned her head to squint through the intact but grimy window into the garage. She saw a tangle of bicycle wheels in the foreground and, farther back, there were dark shapes of automobiles. Despite the appearance it gave to the outside world, the garage was still being used, however sporadically.

How odd. Curious now, Dee looked speculatively at the double row of garages flanking both sides of the mews. Was it possible that they were all still in use?

Carefully, on the lookout now for more grease patches or other signs of current activity, Dee moved on to the next garage. There was no grease here, but Dee noticed that the rusty hinges of the door were well-oiled, so that the door could operate swiftly and soundlessly. The inside of this window was heavily cobwebbed; you'd need a flashlight to see much of anything. Nevertheless, she had an impression of looming shapes in the blackness, giving the lie to the air of abandonment and neglect it otherwise projected.

Dee straightened and was about to test her burgeoning theory against the next garage when she had an abrupt unpleasant sensation of being observed.

She turned away from the window, elaborately casual. Suddenly, it seemed important that she be nothing but an innocent bystander of the most casual and superficial sort. She rubbed her hand and wrist again, ostentatiously flexing it, as though it were the only thing on her mind.

Without a backward glance—or glancing anywhere else—she crossed the mews to the entrance to Connie's shared flat. The street door was still unlocked—perhaps the latch did not work properly; or perhaps Tanya left it that way in case her returning flatmates had lost their keys.

Dee closed the door firmly behind her, hearing the latch snick locked, and leaned against it, feeling as though she had just run a long distance at a speed almost beyond her strength. The stairs looked too steep for comfort, but she took a deep breath and managed them easily.

The flat door *was* tightly closed and she knocked once, then, after a short pause, a second time more loudly. She sensed a change in the quality of the silence behind the door, as though someone was listening to try to determine who was waiting outside.

"Tanya?" she called. "Tanya, it's Mrs. Sawyer. Connie's mother. I'd like to talk to you."

There was no answer but, after a long moment, a key scraped in the lock and the door swung open. Tanya stood there, the Basenji puppy lurking expectantly behind her ankles. He darted forward, tail wagging, uttering muted yodels of recognition.

Oh yes, Dee thought bleakly, stooping to pat him, *a fat lot of good you'd be in an emergency*. She hoped her smile betrayed no trace of this pessimism as she beamed it at Tanya.

"What is it?" Tanya asked nervously. "What's the matter?"

"Can we go inside?" Dee suggested it since Tanya obviously wasn't going to. She moved forward as though the answer were a foregone conclusion.

"Oh . . . yes . . . " Tanya looked as though she wished she had the nerve to bar the doorway. "Come in . . . "

The room was dark, a low-wattage bulb in the one lamp that was lit did little to dispel the gloom. It took a few seconds before Dee's eyes adjusted enough to see that there was someone else in the room, sitting in the corner of the shabby sofa.

"Mrs. Sawyer." He rose to his feet and came forward, extending a hand. "Allow me to introduce myself—" It was obvious to both of them that Tanya wasn't going to bother with introductions. "I'm Giles, Giles Abbott. I was—I *am*—a friend of Connie's."

"How do you do?" Dee was formal, mentally crossing a set of initials off the list from Connie's diary. The initials had recurred frequently. But there was another reason that name was familiar . . .

"Are you—" she asked cautiously— "any relation to Dean Abbott?"

"My father." He dipped his head in admission and, perhaps, mourning.

"How is he?"

"The same, I'm afraid." His head dipped lower, his face and voice remained completely expressionless, betraying no emotion.

"I'm sorry."

"Thank you. But Connie—" He raised his head and stepped back, his eyes met hers with a flash of intimacy that startled her. "I hadn't seen her in class, so I came round to invite her to a concert. Tanya tells me she's still away. But—" he frowned. "You're here. Connie didn't tell me you were coming over. Is there—something wrong?"

"Connie is missing."

"Missing?" He might never have heard the word before. "What do you mean?"

"I mean she's missing. No one has seen her since school broke up for the Easter holiday. She hasn't been in contact with anyone, she hasn't written home . . . "

"Oh!" He grasped the seriousness of the situation at once. "That's not like her."

"Exactly." Dee found herself warming to him; as Connie had warmed. There had been increasingly flattering references to G.A. as the diary had progressed. It was understandable that she had always used initials for him, not wanting him to be identified as the Dean's son if anyone should dip into her diary. Connie's growing interest in him was understandable, too. He was tall and good-looking in a fine-boned English way, and he gave the impression of being more mature than his American contemporaries, Was she looking at the boy who—if fate had been kinder—might have been her future son-in-law?

"But—" he gazed at her earnestly, frowning with concern— "what are you going to do?"

"I'm going to look for her." Abruptly, Dee felt chilled, hearing the words as they must sound to Giles.

"Then you know where she is? If you do, then she isn't really missing, is she?"

Tanya sighed faintly. She had retreated to the shadows at the far side of the room and stood watching them. Even the puppy had caught the general mood and crouched at her feet, subdued.

"You sound like the others," Dee said bitterly. "I've reported her as a missing person, but the police seem to feel it's too early to do anything about it—the little they *can* do, that is. And that—that *Acting* Dean isn't going to act, either. He doesn't *want* to believe me."

"No, he wouldn't," Giles agreed. "It's too bad my father is so ill. He'd have got things moving."

"Everything happens at once." Tanya moved forward slightly. "I've just been telling Giles that Jaycee and Maggie aren't back."

"They must all have gone off together." Giles came to the same initial conclusion that everyone else had reached. "That's the trouble with these on-the-cheap Continental holidays; something goes wrong and it takes ages for word to come through. There may have been an accident—" He broke off, becoming aware that he was adding to Dee's distress.

"Connie hasn't left the country." Dee kept her voice steady. "We've found her passport."

"Good!" Hope was born in his face and died rapidly. "I mean, that narrows the field. Well, it's a start . . . "

"Not much of a one," Dee admitted. "I'm just beginning to realize how big the United Kingdom is. It looks so small and . . . containable . . . on a map, but when you get here even London seems enormous."

"It is," Giles said. "It's one of the biggest cities in the world. Very easy to get lost in . . . " He broke off again, miserably aware that he was losing ground in the tactfulness stakes.

"They might all be back any time now," Tanya offered tentatively, not giving the impression that she really believed it. She had been saying it for so long now that it had become a knee-jerk reaction.

"I'll help you to find Connie," Giles said decisively. "I'll help you all I can. So will Tanya. Er—" His decisiveness began to fade. "Where do you think we should start?"

"I wish I knew."

"Haven't you any idea?" Her admission of weakness seemed to give Giles new strength. "She must have sent you lots of letters, she always seemed to be writing one. Didn't you find any clue in them as to where she might have gone? She must have had favorite places . . . special friends. Don't you have any idea at all?"

"I wish I had."

"But you're here," Giles said, as though that had some deeper significance. "You must have felt you could do something by being here."

"I hoped I could push other people into doing something." Dee shook her head. "I was sure that the authorities—"

"The authorities never do anything until it's too late," Tanya said gloomily. She looked at Dee's face and added hastily, "Or almost too late."

"I'm afraid she's right," Giles said. "It takes a lot to persuade the Powers-That-Be that anything concerning students—short of a demonstration—is serious. They want proof. I take it—" he paused delicately—"you don't have any proof?"

"Only my knowledge of my daughter. I know that Connie would never stop writing home unless—"

"Ah yes," Giles said quickly. "The well-known Mother's Instinct. The authorities don't accept that as evidence."

"So I've discovered. The police as good as suggested that she was only waiting to get out from under my thumb so that she could start leading a wild life."

"No," Giles said. "Not Connie."

"No . . . " Tanya echoed. "Not Connie . . . "

"I'm glad we're all agreed," Dee said. "Now, how do we convince the authorities?"

"Perhaps, if we all went to them together . . . " Tanya let the thought trail off, sensing its hopelessness.

"That's no good," Giles said gently. "We'd be better off

trying to do something on our own. Ask around, talk to her other friends . . . "

"And talk to the friends of the other missing students," Dee said. "If we can get enough information, once we start cross-indexing it, there must be intersecting lines. They ought to give us some kind of clue."

"Right!" Giles said. "Right!" He looked at her uncertainly. "What other missing students?"

"Professor Standfast admitted—much as he hated to— that there were several other students who hadn't returned to their classes yet. He seemed to feel that it explained Connie's absence. He said some students were always late reporting back after the holidays."

"Perhaps, but not this late." Giles frowned, suddenly very much the Dean's son. "Do you mean to say Standfast knows he's got a party of students missing and he isn't doing anything about it?"

"Most especially, he isn't worrying about it," Dee said bitterly. "He claims they'll be returning any time now."

Tanya made a quiet little sound at the back of her throat. It was what she was hoping, too.

"Leave them alone and they'll come home, wagging their tails behind them, eh?" Giles shook his head. "If my father knew that, he'd have a stroke—"

He already had. If he hadn't, Professor Standfast wouldn't be in charge now.

"Oh God!" Giles sank down into a chair, shaking his head dazedly. "It's all too much!"

Dee was abruptly aware of just how young he actually was. About the same age as Connie. The cloak of sophistication had slipped from his shoulders, revealing him as a boy suddenly faced with too much responsibility, too quickly.

"How is your mother?" Dee asked, wondering if she dared broach the subject of an interview with the woman, but feeling guiltily that it might add to his burden.

"Just like my father." He gave a muffled bark that might have been intended to be a sardonic laugh. "Doing as well as can be expected."

"Should I make some tea?" Tanya offered uneasily, out of her depth in the emotional currents surging around her. The puppy whined softly at her feet.

"Not for me, thank you." Dee decided on a strategic retreat. "I have another engagement. I don't want to be late."

"Oh, but I thought you wanted to talk to me—"

"I'll have to see you later, Tanya. And you, too, Giles. Perhaps I could see your mother at the same time." It was worth a try. "But I can't stay any longer—" She dropped the name that she hoped would impress them. "I can't be late meeting Dr. Carson."

"Ah yes, Carson," Giles said thoughtfully. Something in his expression told Dee that the name had not had the impact she intended.

"He's going to help me," Dee said.

"Is he?" Giles nodded judiciously and, with an imperceptible tug, the cloak of sophistication was back in place. "Good . . . good man, Carson."

But there was something slightly peculiar about the way he said it, turning it into a classic example of damning with faint praise.

It left Dee wondering just what was wrong with Dr. Carson.

CHAPTER 19

The pub was comfortably full and the noise level was rising pleasantly, buoyed by bursts of laughter from groups clustered at the long bar. Dee hesitated just inside the door and looked for Dr. Carson. She found him at the bar, talking to a man even shorter and burlier than himself.

Perhaps he sensed someone watching him, for he turned abruptly and spotted her at once. He raised his hand to her, spoke a few words to his companion, and turned and made his way to her.

"I've bagged us a table," he said. "This way."

She followed him through the thick of the crowd. They emerged on the far side of the room where a small circular table on wrought-iron legs had been marked out, almost buried under the untidy heap of his belongings: a briefcase, muffler, gloves and books.

"Just move this." He tossed the pile from the tabletop to the plush-covered seat that ran the length of the wall. "Now, sit down and I'll get you a drink."

"I don't want—" But he was gone again, leaving her to guard the table and his half-empty mug of beer. Was that what was wrong with him, she wondered? Had Giles been trying to warn her that he was an alcoholic and therefore unreliable?

Carson reclaimed his place at the bar, his erstwhile companion moving to one side to make room for him.

Carson spoke to the man briefly and he turned to stare at Dee while Carson placed his order with the bartender.

Dee looked away, suddenly uncomfortable. What had Carson said about her? The man's stare was too bold, too penetrating, too curious, for it to have been anything good. Or was he perhaps sizing up someone he considered a potential rival? Was that what Giles had been trying to tell her about Carson?

"Here we are." Abruptly, Carson was back, placing a glass in front of her and setting another, full, mug beside his partially-finished drink. "How was your afternoon?"

"All right," she answered, then wondered why she had bothered to be so polite. It had not been all right; it had been thoroughly unsatisfactory. Any day in which she had not found Connie was going to be unsatisfactory.

"Mmm." He nodded as though he had read her thoughts. "Well—" He lifted his mug. "Drink up, anyway."

"You said you had the list of names," Dee prompted.

"Impatient, aren't you?" He glanced at her untouched glass.

"She's my daughter."

"Yes." He set down his mug and reached for one of the books, extracting a sheet of paper from between its pages. "Names, home addresses and telephone numbers. Not in any sort of alphabetical order, I'm afraid."

"It doesn't matter." She almost snatched the sheet of paper from him. That was the least of her worries. She read the names:

Alison Thatchpole
Jason Charles (Jaycee) Gale
Margaret Lawrence

Constance Sawyer (She knew that it must be there, but her heart twisted briefly.)

Martin Foster

James Marshall

Henry Daniels

The last name had been crossed off.

"That last one has been accounted for." Carson answered Dee's questioning look. "His mother rang a few days ago and said he was down with flu."

"Oh yes," Dee remembered. "Professor Standfast mentioned him."

"It might even be true." Carson shrugged. "But one would be more inclined to believe it if she'd rung us as soon as term started. It's more likely he just got back from wherever he'd been and she's making excuses for him. He's supposed to resume classes next week."

"How long do you think he's been home?"

"Hard to say." He shrugged again. "At a guess—an educated guess—he probably got home the same day his mother called. She'd have sense enough to know that he ought to report in, especially if he didn't intend to return to classes immediately."

"I want to talk to him!" She half-rose, ready to dash out and hail a taxi. "He's the first to return, he may be able to tell me what happened to the others."

"You'd better telephone first and make sure he's home. It's a long way to Putney."

"Where's the telephone?"

"Over there." He gestured. "Here, you'd better take this."

"I have plenty of change," she said, before noticing that he was offering her a plastic card.

"Perhaps you have," he said, "but the phonecard-operated machines are less likely to be vandalized. Take it just in case."

"Thank you." She accepted the card and moved away. The telephones were in a small passageway leading off from the other end of the bar. She saw the man Carson had been speaking to stare at her as she passed, then he detached himself from the bar and went to join Carson at the table.

All right. With any luck, she'd be able to reach Henry Daniels and make arrangements to go and see him tonight. Then she could leave the pub and stop ruining their evening.

Both telephones were in working order, but someone was already using the phonecard instrument. Good, then she wouldn't have to use Carson's phonecard and be any more beholden to him. She fed coins into the slot and dialed.

The telephone at the other end rang for quite a long while before anyone answered.

"Yes? What is it now?" It was a woman's voice; she sounded very annoyed.

"Mrs. Daniels?"

"Yes. Who is this?" The voice became carefully modulated, cautious.

"I'm Delia Sawyer. You don't know me but—"

"I'm sorry, we never buy anything from telephone solicitations. Good—"

"Please! Don't hang up. I'm not selling anything. I want to talk to Henry. He *is* your son, isn't he?" Dee asked the question hurriedly, hoping that father and son didn't share the same name; the woman sounded like the jealous type.

"My son, Henry? What do you want to talk to him for?"

"It's all rather complicated." Dee dismissed the idea of even trying to explain to this woman. "May I speak to him, please?"

"He isn't here just now. May I take a message?"

"Do you know where I can reach him?" Any message would be too complicated. "Or perhaps you could tell me what time he'll be home and I can call again."

"No, don't do that! One of his mates rang up and he's gone haring off. I don't know where he is or what time he'll be home— but it will be late." The mood had turned waspish. "Too late to be getting telephone calls. Some of us sleep at night, you know."

"Tomorrow, then." Dee resolved to go there in person, no matter how great the distance. It was obvious that Henry's mother did not approve of any of her son's friends and would be no party to putting them in touch with him. The best way to deal with her was to arrive on the doorstep in the morning.

"Hummph!" The receiver slammed down at the other end and the dial tone buzzed in Dee's ear.

As she approached the table, Dee saw that the man from the bar was sitting there, deep in conversation with Dr. Carson. She hesitated, but he was now obviously a member of their party.

The man got to his feet as she reclaimed her seat, but Carson, either more casual or blocked by the table, remained where he was and gave her a nod of acknowledgement. "Any joy?" he asked.

"You were right, he isn't home, His mother claims he's gone out with friends. I think I'll go down first thing in the morning and see if I can catch him before he goes out again." She glanced pointedly at the stranger at their table, she had already noticed that the English weren't good at introductions.

"Oh yes." Surprisingly, Carson took the hint. "Mrs. Sawyer, this is Mr. Thatchpole. Mr. Thatchpole—Mrs. Sawyer."

"Thatchpole?" As they shook hands, the name registered with Dee. She glanced down at the sheet of paper she still clutched.

"That's right—Alison's father," Carson confirmed. "He came down from Birmingham because he hasn't been able to get in touch with her since Easter. I thought it might be a good idea for you two to meet."

"Your girl has gone missing, too, I understand." Thatchpole stared intently into her eyes, as though some explanation might be hidden there. "Do you think they're together?"

"I don't know." She saw that another photocopy of her own list of names and addresses lay on the table before him. Dr. Carson evidently didn't believe in duplication of effort. She wondered if he had taken still more copies in preparation for the moment when the remaining parents began to make inquiries.

"My girl wouldn't go off like that."

"Neither would mine."

"I don't believe any of them would," Carson said. "I checked their records while I was about it. Not one of them has any history of absenteeism. They were all earning good grades with no reason to fear final exams. They were all healthy and outgoing, popular with their peers, with no problems that any of their teachers were aware of. I must admit that I'm beginning to be concerned about them."

"Concerned?" Thatchpole's first clenched. "I should bloody well think you'd be worried out of your mind! I know I am. And I'm sure Mrs. Sawyer is—"

"Mrs. Sawyer is not only worried sick—she's furious!" Dee snapped. "I consider it negligence of the worst sort for the school to ignore the fact that so many students are missing—"

"Oh, now, be fair!" Carson interrupted. "This is only the second week of term and it is not unknown for paragons of virtue—even such as your own dear darlings—to help themselves to a bit of extra holiday. If we went running to the police every time a few students were overdue, we'd make a laughing-stock of ourselves. We're educators—not nannies! By the time students reach University they're considered to be reasonably adult and able to manage their own lives—"

"A very convenient attitude!" Thatchpole sneered. "Saves you a lot of bother, doesn't it? You can all sit around with your eyes closed until the police come and tell you the body's been discovered!"

"Oh!" Dee leaned back, feeling the blood drain from her face. That was what she had been trying not to put into words, not even to herself.

"Eee, I'm sorry. I didn't think—" Thatchpole patted her hand awkwardly. "I didn't mean—"

"Here—" Carson raised her glass to her lips.

"I'm all right . . . " She took a sip, but he'd tilted the glass too sharply and liquid ran down her chin.

"You clumsy bugger!" Thatchpole snarled at Carson. He caught up a paper napkin and dabbed at her chin. "Watch what you're doing!"

"Sorry, terribly sorry." Carson set the glass back on the table.

"It's all right." She took the napkin from Thatchpole—he was fairly clumsy himself—and attended to her own chin. "You didn't say anything that hasn't been haunting me for weeks," she told him.

"Aye." He stared into her eyes again and nodded. "Bound to, isn't it? No wonder they call children hostages to fortune. You have them, you bring them up, you never stop caring for them—but you can't wrap them up in cotton wool and watch over them for ever. You have to let them go out into the world—and you never stop worrying again."

"Never," Dee agreed sadly. "All you can do is tell yourself you've taught them all you can and you mustn't be over-protective—and hope that the worst never happens. Only—"

"Only sometimes it does. Perhaps it has." Thatchpole finished the thought for her. He looked down gloomily at his list of names. "What about these others, then?" he demanded of Carson.

"Two of them share a flat with Mrs. Sawyer's daughter—illicitly, I might add. All of them are supposed to be living in the Halls of Residence."

"My Alison was."

"Oh, no doubt about that," Carson said. No one added: *But it didn't save her.*

"That leaves Martin Foster and James Marshall." Dee consulted her own list. "What about them?"

"As you can see by their home addresses, Foster was from Canada. Marshall was from North Dakota—another one on the Junior Year Abroad Program. We haven't heard anything from their families yet."

"How much longer do you intend to sit around before you decide to contact the families?" Thatchpole was growing belligerent and Dee could not blame him. Dr. Carson was too casual for her liking, as well.

"In another few days we'll send off a delicate inquiry to them." Carson's lips twisted wryly. "It's not unknown for overseas students to drop out and return home without bothering to notify us."

"You hang on to that thought if it makes you feel any better," Thatchpole growled. "But my girl didn't go home and—" he jerked a thumb at Dee— "neither did hers. You'll have to come up with better than that."

"I'm sorry." Abruptly, Carson was no longer so casual. "I only wish I could."

"We'll have to talk to all their friends." Dee began to feel faintly despairing. "If we can find out who they are. Perhaps you could make an announcement in your classes—" she turned hopefully to Carson. "And get a notice posted on the bulletin board—"

"It's a bit early for that," Carson said quickly. "We don't want to start a lot of rumors flying."

"No, you wouldn't, would you?" Thatchpole jeered.

Carson ignored him. "Let me make a few discreet inquiries first."

"I'm going down to talk to Henry Daniels first thing in the morning," Dee said. "He might be our best chance."

"If you can hang on until my early class is over," Carson said, "I'll drive you down. I can pick you up about eleven."

"I'll take her down." Thatchpole glared at him. "I've got a car."

"Good for you." Carson met the challenge. "So have I."

"Why don't you both come along?" It seemed like the best solution to Dee. "Mr. Thatchpole will want to know what's happening and Henry Daniels might talk more easily with Dr. Carson present. Otherwise, he'd have two complete strangers firing questions at him and he might not be willing to answer."

"Right!" Thatchpole said. "We'll go in my car."

"Mine!" Carson disputed.

"I'll leave you two to sort out the details." Dee rose, suddenly exhausted. "I've had a long day and I'm going back to the hotel. I'll see you in the morning."

CHAPTER 20

It was raining, and that was all right, too. Rain intensified the smell of the sea in the air, increasing the feeling of security. The room was beginning to seem more homelike, now that a few sorties around the profusion of local charity shops and second-hand stores had provided it with some personal touches. A small oil painting with a cracked gilded frame replaced the ugly mass-produced sentimental print that had hung on one wall. A row of books had begun marching across the back of the desk; a few of them French phrasebooks and grammars to lull the landlady into continuing to believe that she was attending one of the language schools.

Increasingly, however, she was finding old novels, biographies and memoirs were what she wanted to read—or, possibly, re-read. Sometimes she just held a book in her hands, turning it over, stroking it, wondering if she had been drawn to it because it appealed to her now or because it had been a well-loved favorite in that distant other life. Had she read it before? When? And where?

But she was learning to fill her days so that there was little time for brooding. There was so much to explore here in Brighton, not only the city itself, generously spread wide, but the dozens of neighborhoods, probably once separate villages which had been swept up into the metropolitan environs, each with a distinct character of its own: its own shops, restaurants, High Street and hidden treasures down unexpected lanes. It would take weeks, possibly months, to get to know them all. After that, there were all the other towns and cities along the coast, just a short bus hop away. Yes, her instinct had been right: this was a good place to settle.

Best of all, there was The Job. It wasn't the most sensational job in the world—working in a sandwich shop—but it paid enough to cover the room rent and leave her with a bit over. Also, it was a start; the beginning of a work record. When she moved on to a better job, she would be able to provide a reference and prospective employers would not be so worried about a Work Permit, assuming that someone else had already taken care of that technicality.

There was the prospect of another job, too. The sandwich shop was only open on weekdays, but Mr. Pacelli—after watching her work for a couple of days—had mentioned that his uncle might be able to use an extra waitress at weekends for his restaurant near the sea front. Another salary and, especially, tips, would go a long way towards solving her immediate financial problems.

It would mean she needn't use any more of the fifty-pound notes. They continued to frighten her just by their physical presence, let alone the thought that she might someday be called upon to account for them . . . to return them. They were like an albatross tied round her neck, both in the possession of them and in the fear that they might be stolen from her. It was not safe to carry them around with her all the time, particularly since she had to remove her coat and hang it up while she worked in the sandwich shop. Nor did she feel secure about leaving the money in her room while she was at work. The landlady was entirely too curious. She might not actually steal the money—well, not *all* of it— but if she found it, she would be more curious than ever and might begin asking the questions that couldn't be answered.

Banks asked questions, too.

For the moment, the problem was, if not solved, at least in abeyance. She smiled at the little oil painting on the opposite wall. The brown paper covering the back had been torn when she bought it—and that had given her the idea. She had gone to a stationer's and bought fresh brown paper, scissors and glue. Back in the room, she had stripped off the old torn brown paper. Then she had filled the recess between the canvas back and the edge of the wooden stretcher with the fifty-pound notes, carefully smoothed out to lie flat. They took up less room that way and they fitted into the space in four neat piles as though they had been designed for it. She had tucked a protective layer of brown paper over them and sealed it, then covered the entire back, from edge to edge of the frame, with still more brown paper and glued that firmly in place.

The hiding place would not stand up to a determined professional search, but it ought to be proof enough against a nosey landlady snooping around.

Especially since said landlady had already seen the

painting when Cora brought it home—and dismissed it as unworthy of attention.

"You're going to put *that* up?" The disparaging gaze had swept the bleak winter landscape. "It's not something I'd want on *my* wall. Depressing, I call it."

"Yes, well—" Cora avoided the tear-dribbling eyes of a clown-with-a-painted-sad-smile hanging in the hallway over the landlady's shoulder. "It sort of reminds me of home. In the winter, you know."

"Umm, I suppose so—" The landlady sniffed grudgingly. "It's like that in Canada, I hear. But I know what *I* like . . . "

No, there would be no further interest there.

Cora glanced at her watch, her own watch—but bearing no fond inscription, no initials; useless, except as a means of keeping track of the time—and leaped out of bed. She would be late for work if she didn't hurry. She began flinging on her clothes—no name tags, no exclusive labels, all bought locally; also useless.

At least she didn't have to worry about breakfast. That was another big bonus about working with food; it was always available and, when meals were part of the salary, the salary stretched farther.

All in all, she'd been lucky. So far. She could have done a lot worse.

She tried to ignore the tiny voice that whispered that, at some point in the past, she probably had.

CHAPTER 21

It was raining again. That was all she needed. Dee rose slowly, groggily, and crossed to fill the electric kettle and plug it in. The little sachets of powdered coffee looked more inadequate than ever; she needed a bigger caffeine jolt than they could provide. Perhaps if she used two or three of them at once . . .

Halfway through the cup of coffee, she decided to try to call home again. She had tried when she got in last night, but there had been no answer. Now, however, it would be some ungodly hour of the morning in Connecticut and Hal would almost certainly be home, even though asleep. He could not complain if she disturbed his rest to talk to him about Connie. It might serve to remind him that Connie was his daughter, too.

Already the single ring sounded unfamiliar, she had become so accustomed to the double-ring of English telephones. The long wait before anyone answered was the same though.

"Hello—? Hello—?" Hal was in a temper at being aroused. "Who the hell is calling at this hour? Junior, if you think you're being funny—"

Dee opened her mouth, but no sound came out. There was something about the husk in his voice . . .

There was a female gurgle of laughter in the background, low and voluptuous. Someone thought it was funny.

Hal was aroused, all right, but not in the way she had thought. He had that woman with him—in *her* house. In *her* bed.

"Hello—?" There was a more cautious note in Hal's voice now. Perhaps he had belatedly thought of someone who might be calling him at an unearthly hour . . . from another time zone. "Hello—? Who's there? Who's calling?"

The female laughter gurgled again, louder, insistently, triumphantly. Someone else knew who might be calling at this late hour. Too late.

"Hello—? Is that you, D—"

Dee replaced the receiver quietly.

She waited in the lobby for Dr. Carson and Mr. Thatchpole to come and collect her. She could not bear to remain alone in that room with the telephone.

Even in the lobby, there was no refuge from her thoughts. Hal had brought his other woman into her house. Shamed her in front of the world, the neighbors. Someone was sure to have seen them together, it was inevitable. Was this the first time? Or had he been bringing the woman home every night since his wife had gone to Europe?

No, it wasn't the first time. Hal had betrayed that in his first questions. He'd thought it might be Junior calling— trying to be funny. That meant that Junior was in on the secret, was amused by it. His Old Man, kicking over the traces. Did he care what his mother would think about it? Or did he think that as long as she didn't know, it was all right? Did he imagine she would remain in perpetual ignorance? Or had he become part of the male chauvinist society which assumed a man's right to two wives, the first childhood-sweetheart wife to raise his family and see him through the hard-working days, to be succeeded by the trophy wife, the younger, prettier female who attested to his success?

Dee took a deep breath. There was no sense in getting angry with Junior when it was Hal who was to blame. It was typical of Hal that he had already enlisted Junior on his side.

Side . . . were they lining up and taking sides now? Had it come to that? And was she left with just Connie on her side? Connie, another woman, one of the interchangeable females whose opinions really did not matter.

For a moment, her fighting spirit flared. She ought to get on the next flight, burst into the house and confront them. Fight for Hal, as the other woman was doing. But . . . was he worth fighting for? Perhaps once he might have been, but he was now a proven liar and cheat. Whatever had been between them in the beginning had been blurred and eroded by the intervening years.

Also . . . what would happen to Connie if she raced back to fight for Hal? Connie, whether dead or alive, was lost and alone in a strange country. Only her mother was going to worry about her, fight for her, hunt for her.

Her husband . . . or her daughter? Was the choice really as simple and primitive as that? Or was there a choice at all? Was she flattering herself about her ability to retrieve the situation? Perhaps she had already lost Hal. And Connie was lost, too, in a different way.

Lost . . . everything, everyone she had worked for and loved during the long years of her marriage. Swept away . . . leaving her to start a new life on her own. Or . . . to poke around in the rubble that was left, seeking something she could save. Connie . . .

"Are you all right, Mrs. Sawyer?"

"Oh!" She hadn't heard him approach. She opened her eyes and forced a smile. "Yes, thank you, Mr. . . . Thatchpole."

"Why don't you make it Stan? We've got too much in common to be so formal."

"Yes, and I'm Dee." Her smile was a little brighter. Another ally.

"That teacher not here yet?" He frowned around the lobby. "Taking his time about it, isn't he? He's the one who said eleven o'clock."

"Perhaps he's been delayed . . . "

"We'll take *my* car." Stan Thatchpole made it an order. "I saw his last night. Disgraceful old banger, full of dents. More the sort you'd expect of a student than a teacher. You don't want to be seen in a mobile garbage tip like that."

"It doesn't matter." She closed her eyes again.

"Here—" He touched her shoulder tentatively. "You don't want to worry like that. We'll find them, both of them. And we'll give them a right royal roasting for throwing such a scare into us. And then we'll have a good laugh about it and I'll take us all out to dinner at the best restaurant in town. You'll see."

"I hope so." There was nothing else to say; he was trying to convince himself as much as her.

"It's about time!" The trumpeted challenge made her open her eyes to find, as she had expected, that Dr. Carson had arrived.

"Sorry," Carson apologized perfunctorily. "Had a spot of bother starting my car. Battery's a bit flat."

"I should think so! Anybody can see it doesn't get

proper care. No matter, we're taking mine, anyway. I wouldn't trust myself to that bucket of rust you've got."

"Oh, very well." Surprisingly, after all his arguments last night, Dr. Carson capitulated without a struggle. Perhaps his own car no longer looked so good to him in the light of day, or what passed for day this morning. And, of course, wet weather always reacted badly with old cars.

"Come on, then, let's get started. We've wasted enough time." Thatchpole shepherded them out of the hotel and led them to an underground car park a short distance away.

"You wait here," he directed. "I'll go down and get it." He seemed unconcerned about leaving them standing in the rain.

"Probably hasn't got the best parking place in the garage—" Carson revealed a catty streak— "and doesn't want us to know it."

"He won't be long." Dee hoped it was true. She hadn't thought about an umbrella when she packed, but perhaps she ought to buy one.

"Here—" Carson unfurled his umbrella and opened it with a flourish somewhat marred by the fact that a spoke poked out, a denuded skeletal rib, and the material strained in a way that suggested the two flanking ribs were about to be stripped at any moment. He held it over her head twirling it slightly so that the bare spoke was at the back.

"Thank you." It was a kind gesture, but he seemed to be as careless with his umbrella as with his car. They stood together in a silence which, in other circumstances, might have been companionable.

"I knew it!" Carson exclaimed as a sleek grey car came

into view, its radiator ornament the classic dipped lady with floating draperies.

"Get in." Carson hurriedly closed the umbrella, but the trace of a smirk on Thatchpole's lips meant that it was too late.

Dee got into the passenger seat beside Thatchpole, feeling it was better to keep them as far apart as possible.

"Fasten your seat-belt," he said. "It's the law here. The ones in the back seat don't have to bother."

Dr. Carson fastened his seat-belt anyway, which was just as well, for Thatchpole was given to flying starts, they discovered. He demonstrated the trait as every red light changed to green throughout the entire journey.

Dee heard Carson's barely-muffled sigh of relief as they crossed the Thames at Putney Bridge.

"Just about there now," Thatchpole said. "What was that address again?"

"Hold on, I've got an A-Z here. It's all mapped out." Carson pulled the book of maps from his pocket. "Drive on, I'll navigate."

"Bloody knowall!" Thatchpole muttered under his breath, but continued to drive while Carson called out directions. Several turnings later they appeared to have arrived.

"Turn right, right here. This is the street. Slowly now . . . we want number thirty-five . . . "

It was a pretty little house with a low brick wall enclosing a front garden bright with spring flowers, but there was something odd about it. Thatchpole drew up, blocking the short driveway that led to the garage abutting the house.

"I don't like the look of that," Thatchpole said softly.

"What?" Dee hadn't placed what seemed wrong.

"Curtains still drawn. And it's gone noon."

"Do you think we ought to park just here?" Carson asked uneasily.

"I've a feeling we won't be long." Thatchpole released his seat-belt and opened his door. The others followed suit.

They went up the path together. It was Thatchpole who rang the doorbell, barely touching it. The answering chimes from the other side seemed equally subdued. They waited. Eventually Thatchpole pressed the doorbell again, more firmly. The chimes still seemed distant and without urgency, informing rather than summoning.

"There may not be anyone home," Dec almost whispered.

"They're in there." Thatchpole sounded certain. "They'll come in their own good time." She was conscious that his gaze met Carson's over her head; some coded message was exchanged.

"Oh!" The door opened so abruptly and silently that Dee was startled. The woman standing there was not at all what she had pictured during last night's telephone conversation. This was a dry husk of a woman whose clothes seemed too big for her. She gazed at them without curiosity, waiting to hear what they had to say.

"Mrs. Daniels—?" Dee took the initiative, the men seemed to have gone speechless. "I'm Delia Sawyer, we spoke last night. I told you I'd come over this morning—" Dee broke off uneasily. The woman wasn't reacting at all.

"Don't you remember? I called to talk to Henry, but he wasn't home. I'd said I'd come to see him today—"

"Henry?" The blank eyes looked at her unseeingly. "Oh no, I'm afraid you can't see Henry. Not now. Henry isn't here any more."

"Well—" It was going to be the wrong thing to say. Something warned Dee that whatever she said was going to be wrong. Out of the corner of her eyes, she saw Carson make a protective gesture, as though to shield her. "Where is he?"

"He isn't here. No—" The woman shook her head, then, like a broken mechanical toy, went on shaking it. "No, Henry never came home last night. It wasn't his fault—" She seemed anxious to avert some implied criticism of her son.

"He tried. He almost made it. He got as far as the corner—" She gestured vaguely. "And then—and then. Hit-and-run, the police said it was. Never had a chance—"

"I'm sorry." Dee felt numbed and not just with pity for the woman. She hadn't realized how much she had been depending on this being a lead to Connie.

"Oh yes. It was his first night out after all that time with the flu. I didn't want him to go out. I told him it was too soon, but he said he had to talk to his friend, it was important. He worried too much about his friends and not enough about himself." It seemed that the voice mechanism of the automaton was broken, too. Dee had the feeling that this was not the first time she had told this story, nor would it be the last; the woman was doomed to go on and on repeating it to anyone who would listen, trying to understand, trying to come to terms with what had happened.

"Henry should have taken better care of himself after such a nasty bout of flu. He even came back early from his holiday trip because of it and went straight to bed. That wasn't like him. He stayed in bed for days, shivering and shaking, too sick to talk. Refused to have the doctor, too, said there was nothing a doctor could do that I couldn't do. True enough, I nursed him through chicken pox, measles, broken bones—" She broke off, staring into some unimaginable pit of hell.

"Almost all his bones were broken, the hospital said. They tried their best, but they couldn't save him. And there was nothing I could do. Nothing at all. I'd have done anything, but—"

"Is there anything we can do?" Carson asked.

"You?" The ghost of a smile twitched across her mouth. "Oh no. There's nothing anyone can do." Still looking at some horror beyond them, she turned and drifted down the hallway, leaving the door open behind her.

"Shouldn't we—?" Dee started forward, but Thatchpole caught her arm, stopping her.

"There'll be somebody with her," he said. "Neighbors or the rest of the family. She'll be all right."

She wouldn't be. Dee knew that, watching her drift aimlessly down the hallway, another woman who had had her life suddenly wrenched out from underneath her. Bereft, most of her reason for living gone . . . lost . . .

Thatchpole reached out and gently closed the front door, leaving them standing on the doorstep. "Nothing more we can do here, then.

"Nothing . . . " Dee echoed. Nothing, as the woman had said. It was all over for her son, for her.

"Come away." Thatchpole's grip tightened on her arm, reminding her that he had just watched his hopes vanish, too.

CHAPTER 22

It had worked. Or at least partially worked. So far. Keeping the Sawyer woman in his sights was going to be the way to find that bitch of a daughter of hers. Eventually. If she were to be found.

For a moment his mind toyed longingly with the daydream that Connie Sawyer might have been wounded, after all, and had crawled away to die in some obscure alleyway. Or fallen into the river and been carried out to sea.

But you couldn't depend on luck like that. It was dangerous to depend on luck at all. He'd learned that now. Things had been going so well he'd thought he was invulnerable.

Then things had begun going wrong—so suddenly and so violently that he still had trouble believing it. Fortunately, so had Henry.

Once he'd been put on to Henry's trail—and that was thanks to the Sawyer woman—there had been no trouble contacting him, coaxing him out of the fortress home guarded by that dragon of a mother. Henry had been only too anxious for a meeting, eager to be assured that he hadn't seen what he knew he had seen. The mere hint that it had all been some sort of elaborately stage-managed practical joke had brought Henry trotting to the rendezvous, ready to doubt the evidence of his senses in favor of the big comforting lie.

Any explanation will suffice when you're preaching to those who want to believe. It would only be later, at home, when he had time to go over it mentally, that Henry would begin to spot the holes in the story. But that didn't matter, because Henry wasn't going to reach home again.

Meanwhile, he'd learned what he set out to learn: Henry didn't know where Connie was, either.

As he'd thought, Connie and Henry had got out together. But, in the darkness and the river mist, they had become separated. Henry had searched for her a while— Henry had skated over that bit very quickly. Obviously, he hadn't searched for too long in his panic to get away himself, nor would he have dared to call her name in case someone else was out there in the mist searching for both of them.

After that, Henry had said vaguely, he had wandered around for a few days. Until his money ran out and he could think of nothing better to do than to return home to his mother. He hadn't been feeling at all well by then, he was pretty sure he had flu—all those chills and fevers— especially chills. But he'd been feeling better (hadn't we all?) as the days had gone by and nothing had . . . well . . . happened.

That reinforced the argument: Not that you were hallucinating, old boy, but . . .

Yah, sure! Henry would gladly have admitted to hallucinating. It had been such a nightmare . . .

But it was all done with mirrors . . . or something. The fact that so much time had passed and nothing had . . . happened . . . was surely proof of that? Another drink?

Yah, sure! To both suggestions. Henry had relaxed; more than relaxed, deflated like a pricked balloon under the jointly soothing influences of alcohol and hearing what he wanted to hear. He'd been startled out of his skin by the . . . the stage effects. They'd been so lifelike . . . or deathlike . . .

Well, they were supposed to be, weren't they? A good joke on one and all. (But the bulldozers were creeping forward inexorably. The wrecking ball swung nearer and nearer. It wouldn't be long now. And there must be no witnesses left to point an accusing finger. To testify . . .)

But . . . but . . . Henry was frowning with concentration, trying to mobilize his thoughts. But . . . where were the others? Why hadn't he heard from them?

Taking a bit of extra holiday, of course. You know how that one goes, don't you? Doing a bit of it yourself.

Yah, but . . . but . . . Connie. Where was Connie?

Ah, I asked you first. Not to worry, she's due to turn up any time now. Classes have started, after all. You *are* coming back to class?

Yah, sure. Next week, I promise. Feeling a lot better now. Ready to put the old nose to the grindstone again.

Good! Er, see here (portentous frown at watch) I have another appointment. It's nearly closing time, in any case. Drink up and I'll drop you off. Can't go all the way to the door, if you don't mind. But I can leave you a street or two away. That will be all right, won't it?

Of course, it would. Henry had been too flattered by the attention to protest, too fuddled to be suspicious.

He never even looked over his shoulder when he heard the car accelerate behind him.

CHAPTER 23

The last person Dee expected to hear from was Professor Justin Standfast. Yet, there he was, on the end of the line.

"Mrs. Sawyer, I'm so glad. I've reached you. I wasn't sure you'd still be here."

"I shall be here until I've found my daughter."

"Ah yes. You've had no luck, er, success then?"

"Not yet. Not unless you have any information for me."

"Ah, not perhaps information as such . . . in the way that you mean it, but . . . I think we should discuss this matter further."

"I would welcome that, Professor Standfast," Dee said evenly. "As soon as possible."

"I agree. I can see you this afternoon." Suddenly, he was conferring a favor. "In my office at four o'clock. I trust that will be convenient?" He didn't care whether it was or not; there was a take-it-or-leave-it note in his voice.

"That will be fine." Dee took it; she had no choice.

"I will see you then." He was the Dean, oh definitely the Dean, arranging an appointment with a recalcitrant student. "Goodbye."

"I'll have—" But he had already cut her off. She smiled, the onus was now upon him. If he protested, she could say that she had been just about to mention it to him, but he had hung up on her. Good.

It would take him off-guard when she arrived in company with Mr. Stanley Thatchpole—another concerned parent. An English parent, who wouldn't be so easily browbeaten as some foreign female. Professor Standfast was about to have a nasty shock—and not before time.

Feeling cheered for the second time that day, Dee turned to a consideration of her meager wardrobe to try to find something decent enough to change into for a late lunch with Stan Thatchpole, who was waiting for her downstairs in the lobby.

The first time she had been cheered today had been earlier, after Carson had left them to hurry back to the college for his next class. Thatchpole had driven them back from Putney to the West End, but stopped her as she had been about to follow Carson out of the Rolls-Royce.

"Hang on a bit—" His hand had closed firmly around her arm. "*You* don't have to go and lecture to a pack of young muckers. Let's put our heads together and start comparing notes. We might be able to come up with something."

"All right." She relaxed back into the seat thankfully, aware of Carson's disapproval, but uncaring. She had been hoping for an opportunity to talk to Thatchpole privately; if he hadn't made the overture, she would have telephoned him later and suggested it. They had a lot to talk about and they could talk more uninhibitedly without the presence of someone who might be more worried about the reputation of the school.

"I'll ring you later." Carson divided an uneasy glance between them, making it unclear which one he was addressing.

"You do that." Thatchpole set the car into motion and rolled out into the line of traffic, leaving Carson standing on the curb, looking after them impotently. "Bit of a wimp, that one, I'd say," he confided to Dee.

"Mmm," Dee murmured noncommittally. Was that what Giles had been trying to tell her about Carson: that he was a complete wimp? Adequate in the classroom, perhaps, but not to be depended upon out in the real world when the going got rough?

"We can talk just as well over a meal as not." There could be no doubt that Thatchpole was in command of the real world. "The Savoy Grill suit you?"

"I'm not hungry," Dee said.

"Well, I am." Thatchpole turned the car towards the Thames. "Don't fret," he added, with unexpected sensitivity. "We'll find them."

"But we shouldn't be wasting time. A restaurant will take too long. We should be *doing* something! We should—" With dismay, she heard the tears trembling in her voice. "We should be checking the hospitals, the—" She could not finish.

"It's been done." He reached into his breast pocket and pulled out his handkerchief. "I had my secretary ring them all before I came down here. It's all right, the girls aren't there. Neither yours nor mine. No unidentified patients in any of them right now; no, nor haven't been for months."

"But—" She took the handkerchief. "But that's just London. There are so many other cities—"

"Aye, but it's a start." He glanced at her. "Doesn't that make you feel a little better?"

"Yes and no." It was a relief to feel that she could be honest with this man; he knew what she was going through. She snivelled into his handkerchief shamelessly.

"We've got to stick together through this." He voiced her own thoughts. "Work together, pool our information.

I've found out about the hospitals and—" his voice hardened— "the morgues. You've approached it from the other end and been questioning your daughter's friends. I'd like to meet those friends and ask them some questions of my own. They must have known Alison, too."

"That's right!" She blew her nose and dabbed at her eyes, trying to become businesslike again. "Certainly Heidi would. They were both in the Princess Louise Hall. Heidi realized that Connie was missing, but she didn't know about Alison. And I only asked about Connie. I didn't know about Alison, either."

"And it wouldn't have meant much to you if you had," he said flatly. "You were only concerned with your own girl, as was right and proper. And I was only concerned with mine, but now it looks as though—" He broke off to concentrate all his energies on avoiding a suicidal motorcyclist. His language for the next few seconds was lurid and heartfelt.

"Pardon my French," he apologized, "but I don't know why they allow those buggers a license. Nothing but a danger to everybody else on the road. Yes—" he swerved again as a racing bike swept past them—"and that goes for those damned bicycles, too."

"They seem to be very popular." She watched the bike weaving through the traffic. "I've seen a lot of them around."

"Aye, and they cost a packet, too! I bought one for Alison, so I know. Ten-speed bikes! Mountain bikes!" He snorted. "And then she had it stolen first crack out of the box. It's a big racket, stealing those bikes. I wouldn't replace it. Told her to save up her pennies and buy some proper wheels." His voice thickened. "I wish now—"

"That won't help." For the moment, Dee was stronger.

"We can't go around feeling guilty about every little thing we did or didn't do."

"You're right." He turned to look at her and she saw the trace of a frown appear on his forehead. "Mmm, and you might be right about wasting time at the Savoy Grill, too. Perhaps we ought to go to some fast-food place. And, mmm, perhaps you'd like me to stop at your hotel first, so that you can freshen up a bit?"

"Yes." She understood that she must sound a lot better than she looked, tearstained and distraught. "That's a good idea. I'd like to freshen up and change."

How fortunate that she had come back to the hotel; otherwise she would have missed the call from Professor Standfast. Whatever he wanted to see her about, she could better face if she knew she looked her best.

But . . . she had forgotten to send her travelling suit down for pressing. It hung in the closet as creased and wrinkled as when she had taken it off.

The trouser suit was past its prime and she suspected that Professor Standfast would disapprove of it, anyway. One of the blouses she had packed did not really go with anything else and she had not noticed the spot on the other. She had packed in a hurry and clothes had not seemed to matter. She was going to hunt for Connie, not participate in a style show.

She had conceived a sudden hatred for the outfit she was wearing: an aura of bad news seemed to cling to it. She did not want to wear it to the interview with Professor Standfast lest it attract more bad news, as some materials attracted lint.

That left her with . . . nothing to wear.

An idea occurred to her and would not go away.

Reluctantly, tentatively, she pulled out Connie's suitcase and opened it. Yes, she had remembered correctly.

The maroon cardigan jacket had a matching long-sleeved sweater, both in finest lambswool. There was a plaid woollen skirt with a thin maroon stripe the exact shade of the twin-set. The outfit was as crisp and fresh as the day it had been bought. Perhaps it had never been worn; perhaps Connie had been saving it for a special occasion.

Tears threatened for an instant but she blinked them away. Connie was not dead and it would be silly to treat her clothes as sacrosanct. She and Connie had often borrowed each other's clothes before. To wear these now would be a pledge to the future, an assurance that the old customs were still in force, that Connie was still alive . . .

Professor Justin Standfast was taken aback to find that Dee was accompanied by reinforcements. Taken aback and displeased.

"Mrs. Sawyer." He nodded to her coldly, not advancing from behind his desk nor offering his hand. He had obviously shot his bolt when he rose as she entered. "And, er—?" He looked even more coldly at Thatchpole.

"Thatchpole, Stanley Thatchpole." His glare lowered the temperature as well. "Alison Thatchpole's father."

"Ah yes." The Acting Dean glared at Dee as though she had conjured Stanley Thatchpole out of thin air just to annoy him.

"*My* daughter is missing, too." Thatchpole underlined his interest, in case Standfast hadn't noticed the name. "What are you going to do about it?"

"Sit down." Justin Standfast dropped into his own chair, gesturing to them to do the same. There was only one chair placed in front of his desk. Thatchpole motioned Dee into it, collected another chair from the far side of the room, brought it over and slammed it down beside Dee's.

Professor Standfast winced and glared at him. Thatchpole glared back.

"You wanted to see me, Professor Standfast?" Dee broke up the glaring match. "You said you had fresh information. What is it?"

"Ah yes. Yes." Professor Standfast was never going to approve of her. She rushed things. She tried to lead the conversation. She was unsatisfactory in every way. Unfortunately, she was a concerned parent and must be humored. But not very much.

"I understand—" first, he intended to make his displeasure felt—"I understand that you have been asking questions. Upsetting the students. Involving the staff." He frowned portentously. "I might go so far as to say that you have suborned the staff. Dr. Carson is completely unauthorized to pry into departmental records."

Dee stared at him, radiating cold defiance. She would not be treated as though she were one of his students sent in for discipline.

Thatchpole made a low growling noise deep in his throat.

"Yes, well . . ." Professor Standfast seemed to realize that he had lost his audience and veered sharply on to another tack. "I thought you might like to see this—"

He took up a piece of paper from his desk and brandished it at her. "It's from one of the students you continue to categorize as 'missing'— erk!" He ended in a squawk as Stanley Thatchpole leaned across the desk and tore it from his hands.

"Foster." Thatchpole held the letter so that Dee could see it, too. "The Canadian one."

Together they read the somewhat incoherent phrases that explained that Martin Foster had had to return hurriedly to Toronto because of a serious illness in the family. He did not expect to be able to come back to England and would resume his studies at McGill as soon as family circumstances permitted.

"You see—" Professor Standfast tried to pretend that his feathers were unruffled—"I have no doubt at all that our next communication will be from North Dakota. Unless—" he shot a malevolent glance at Dee— "it's from Connecticut."

"That's not true!" Dee was barely conscious of Thatchpole's restraining hand as she surged to her feet,

"Quite right!" Thatchpole faced the Acting Dean with cold fury. "There's no one ill in Mrs. Sawyer's family. Nor in mine. You'll have to come up with better than that."

"I am merely pointing out—" Professor Standfast spoke with injured dignity—"that one more student has been accounted for. The others, whatever their excuses, will undoubtedly be reporting in over the course of the next few days. There is no need for the hysteria—" he looked at Dee icily—"that has been displayed."

"Maybe you'd like to tell *me* I'm hysterical?" Thatchpole challenged, even more icily. "Go ahead, I'm waiting. Let's hear you say it!"

"Really, this is absurd!" Professor Standfast had gone a deep mottled red. "*I* am the Dean! You must allow me to—"

"The *Acting* Dean," Dee reminded him. "How *is* Dean Abbott?"

"He is improving . . . slowly. And that is another point. You have been upsetting young Giles. He has quite enough on his plate at the moment without being drawn into your affairs. He was caught trying to gain access to confidential files because of your interference—"

"I didn't ask him to!" Dee flared. "He offered to help. He was—*is*—a friend of Connie's."

"That is no excuse! Giles does not have the right to harass the office staff, throwing his dubious weight around as the Dean's son." Professor Standfast appeared to remember something pleasant, he almost smiled. "Particularly as it is highly unlikely that Dean Abbott will be able to resume his duties for quite some time to come. Even if he were to make a complete recovery, Giles would have graduated by then."

And Professor Standfast, if he played his cards right and all went well, would be the official Dean.

"Now that I have clarified the situation—" Acting Dean Standfast held out his hand for the letter Thatchpole was still holding—"I hope you will—"

"Not so fast!" Thatchpole was not prepared to let him terminate the interview at his convenience. "You've clarified nothing except the fact that Mrs. Sawyer's investigations are making you uncomfortable. We still want to know what's happened to our daughters. If you don't like dealing with us, wait until we've hired a private detective to represent us."

"I cannot stop you if you wish to persist in this folly." But Standfast had gone pale, obviously envisioning shoot-outs on the campus. "In fact, I most sincerely hope that you find out what has happened to your daughters." Standfast had retrieved the letter now and rose to his feet, concluding the interview.

"However, you will not, I repeat *not*, do so by continuing to harass the staff and students. If you do, I shall be forced to issue instructions that you are *persona non grata*—and that will also hold true for any emissary you may commission."

"You're storing up a lot of trouble for yourself," Thatchpole growled.

"Threats are useless, as is your continued presence on these premises. You will find that whatever happened to your daughters—if anything—happened off-campus and as a direct result of their extra-curricular activities. Miss Evans—"

Unseen, he had pressed a buzzer at some point during his peroration. His secretary stood in the doorway now, awaiting his instructions.

"Miss Evans, kindly see these people out." *All the way out* was clearly implied.

However, his secretary clearly did not feel that her duties encompassed those of a bouncer and was content to lead them to the top of the stairs and watch as they descended to the lobby.

"If it's the last thing I do, I'll see that one isn't appointed Dean," Thatchpole vowed in a towering fury. He was not accustomed to being treated like that. "He may think he's riding high now but—"

"Connie! Connie!" Dee heard running footsteps, then felt herself being swung around and crushed in a pair of iron arms. "Oh God! I thought—"

Abruptly, the arms fell away. "Oh God!" Giles said again. "It isn't you! I—I'm most terribly sorry, Mrs. Sawyer." He stepped back several paces. "But—" He looked Dee up and down. "But—"

"Yes," Dee said. "I borrowed Connie's clothes. I'm

sorry. I never meant to upset anyone. I didn't think you'd know—"

"I was with her when she bought them." Giles swept an arm across his forehead, the gold of his watch glinting blindingly as the sun caught it. "She tried them on for my approval. That was our joke," he added hastily. "She was going to buy them anyway, she didn't need my approval. Then she came over to the Men's Department with me while I bought this jacket—" He brushed at the butter-soft leather.

"It's very nice." Dee couldn't think of anything else to say. "She must have approved—"

"She loved it. She threatened to have it off me—Oh God!"

"Another joke." Dee nodded, recognizing the intimacy that had been growing between them, marked by their own private jokes. Once, she and Hal—She shook herself mentally, refusing to give way to the nostalgia.

"I was wearing it today—" Giles looked down at the jacket unseeingly—"because it seemed to make her feel nearer. Then, when I saw you from the back, I thought—"

"Yes," Dee said. What he had thought had been only too clear.

"But what are you doing here?" His face brightened. "Have you learned anything new?"

"No," Thatchpole said. "Even though that Standfast tried to teach us our place! Of all the rude, arrogant, overbearing—"

"I know," Giles said. "I wish my father—"

"He's improving, I hear," Dee said. "That must be a great relief to you."

"It is!" Giles managed a smile. "In fact, I'm on my way to see him now. They say he's recovering consciousness for short periods. I'm meeting my mother and sisters at the hospital. But I wanted to talk to you—"

"Aye, and we want to get our heads together with you and the rest of the girls' friends," Thatchpole said.

"Why don't you come round to my hotel later?" Dee suggested. "Meanwhile, I'll try to get hold of Tanya and Heidi and have them there, too. And if you can think of anyone else, bring them along."

"Fine, I'll do that." Giles moved away, still smiling into Dee's eyes. She wondered if he realized that he had avoided looking at her—Connie's—clothes, since those first moments of disappointment when he had been more shaken than he cared to admit to himself. "What time?"

"Say, sevenish," Thatchpole decided. "I'll lay on some sandwiches and coffee. We can get down to business then."

Giles nodded and ran down the front steps with a parting wave. Thatchpole looked after him thoughtfully. "Does all right for himself, that one," he said cryptically, then sighed. "I suppose we'll have to invite Carson, too."

CHAPTER 24

She had noticed him watching her for half the morning, returning to the counter repeatedly. He had worked his way through four sandwiches, four cups of coffee, two bottles of orange juice and one of mineral water, all ordered separately. He lingered a little longer each time. She found that she didn't really mind.

When she had time, she must try to analyze this reaction. Usually, she became frightened and uneasy when anyone paid too much attention to her. But not this time.

Was it because he wasn't English? Nor even American or Canadian? He was simply a young, lonely foreign student looking for a friend. He represented no danger, no menace.

Well, why not? She could use a friend herself. Not a claustrophobic confide-everything intimate, but more a casual companion to go to the movies with, or dinner, or the new show at the Theater Royal. Perhaps that was all he wanted, too. If so, they were in business.

She smiled at him as he approached the counter again, having thought of something else he could order. But there wouldn't be any dinner on offer tonight—it would be amazing if he could force down any more food before lunch-time tomorrow. She could not hold back a giggle as he leaned on the glass case.

"I am funny?" He was not as wounded as he pretended.

"Just a little bit." She giggled again. "Do you mind?"

"Not when you have the so-charming laugh. I am happy to amuse you." He exaggerated a bow, clowning shamelessly now, delighted that the ice was broken.

She shouldn't keep laughing, but she couldn't help it. It had been a long time since she had felt so deliciously light-hearted. Perhaps she was slightly hysterical? No, he *was* charming, charm oozed from every pore. What fun it would be to explore the city with him, to view the world through his eyes.

"Please, do not stop laughing." Those eyes were rolling extravagantly now, playing up to her. "I love to hear you. Just as I love to see you build the sandwich."

"Make—" she said automatically. "Make a sandwich."

"Yes, make. You see? I need the help with my English. Perhaps you would be so kind and help me?"

"Perhaps I would." She regarded him thoughtfully. "If I knew who you were."

"Forgive me." He sobered instantly. "I am André Jourdain. From Paris. And you are—"

"I'm Co—Cora, Cora Trent." Would he notice that she did not mention her city of origin?

"You're French," she added quickly, covering her reticence with a delighted smile. "How nice."

It was better than nice, it was wonderful. Every instinct told her that she could relax and be herself—what she knew of herself— with him. (Why? Why was she so deeply wary of the English boys who had tried to strike up an acquaintance with her, like the hotel clerk? Why did she mistrust them so?)

"I am glad you like. I am here to study English, but the Language School—" he made a face—"it is full of foreigners. I am not able to have the normal English speech with them."

"Colloquial," she said. "You mean colloquial English."

"I do?" He frowned, perhaps the word was a bit advanced for his vocabulary.

"Conversational English," she amended.

"Yes. I cannot have the English conversation with them because they are not able and they have the accents—all different, Greek, Spanish, even Provincial French. Only the teachers talk well and they do not have the time to sit and talk with a sandwich, a beer." He looked at her soulfully. "I need the English friend."

"Well . . ." She preferred him clowning. Even the hint of a possible romance was more than she cared to contemplate. For all she knew, she was married.

She hadn't thought of that before! She waited for some signal from her subconscious, but nothing happened. No reaction at all, especially not the instinctive comforting laughter that had seized her when she had come up with a really outrageous idea. Was she married? To someone awful? Was that why she was so afraid of English men?

"Please? After you finish here, we go for walk? You will tell me the names of flowers—" Sensitive to her mood, he was clowning again. "You will correct my language and help your stupid friend."

"All right . . ." Why not? The world arranged itself in twosomes; as half of a pair, she would be less conspicuous. Better still, if the landlady saw André, it would add to her certainty that Cora was attending a language school and making friends with her fellow students.

"Good!" He beamed at her. "I will wait for you to finish and—" he looked over her shoulder and added hastily— "and I will have another coffee, please."

She looked over her shoulder and caught Mr. Pacelli trying to hide a smile. He had emerged from the back carrying the fresh tub of tuna fish salad he had prepared in the basement kitchen.

"Here—" Mr. Pacelli removed the depleted tub of tuna fish salad and slotted the new one in its place. "Nice and fresh for the lunch-hour rush. I'll just get rid of this old stuff."

"You ought to just scrape it on to the top of the new tub," Cora said. "It's still pretty fresh."

"No, no." He scraped it out on to a saucer instead, elaborately casual. "It's practically stale, only fit for a stray cat."

By the merest coincidence, Cora had noticed, there just happened to be a stray cat lurking by the doorway of the shop. She had been watching with amusement for the past few days as Mr. Pacelli and the black-and-white cat conducted their flirtation. The cat was not going to be a stray for much longer and both of them knew it.

"It doesn't do any harm to have a cat look in once in a while." Mr. Pacelli carried the saucer over and set it down just inside the door, then he opened the door. "Just the smell of them helps keep the mice away. I thought I heard a mouse down in the kitchen the other day."

The cat strolled in and sniffed at the saucer, then rubbed against Mr. Pacelli's ankles before settling down to eat.

"It's not as though we could lay down poison or anything," Mr. Pacelli said defensively, trying to convince no one but himself. "It wouldn't be safe. You can't be too careful when you're working with food."

"I have seen many cats in restaurants here," André said obligingly. "There is problems with mice near water. Rats, too."

"Oh yes, restaurants—that reminds me." Mr. Pacelli turned to Cora. "I spoke to my uncle. He can use you this weekend. Tonight, tomorrow and Sunday, that all right with you?"

"Sounds fine," Cora said cheerfully.

"He'll provide a uniform. You can get an idea of the routine tonight. Then tomorrow night the place is closed to the public, he's got a big Italian wedding celebration. That will really break you in!"

"That's OK," Cora said. "I'm not afraid of hard work."

"No, I've noticed." Mr. Pacelli grinned and winked. "But take some time out for fun, too. All work and no play—no good."

She was annoyed to find herself blushing. So he *had* heard what André had been saying.

"That is what I tell her." André grinned back at him.

"If he doesn't treat you right," Mr. Pacelli said, "I got a couple of cousins—just right for a nice girl like you."

"I treat her right!" André said indignantly. "I promise."

Cora smiled at both of them. A feeling of well-being swept over her. She felt safe with both of them—yes, and with Mr. Pacelli's unknown Italian relatives, too. And André's French relatives, if she ever met them. They wouldn't hurt her.

The smile faded. Who *had* hurt her? Was that why she was afraid of English men?

CHAPTER 25

The academic world was a small one, especially within its own environs. As they left the building, they saw Dr. Carson driving slowly past, obviously looking for a place to park.

"Speak of the devil," Thatchpole growled, waving him down.

Carson waved back and halted beside an already-parked car. "Can I give you a lift?" he called cheerily.

"In *that*?" Thatchpole's contempt grew with every sighting of the battered little saloon.

"We can't all be big Midlands industrialists with Rolls-Royces. Someone has to do some educating and provide the fodder for your dark satanic mills."

"I'm not falling for that one," Thatchpole said. "The mills he meant were educational—colleges." In revenge, he inspected the car more closely. "What have you been doing? You've added more dents since the last time I saw this."

"Just unlucky, I guess. Are you getting in? I can't stay double-parked like this. There's a traffic warden coming."

"It's against my better judgement." Thatchpole wrenched open the door after a brief struggle and helped Dee inside. "For God's sake, drive carefully and try not to hit anything else."

Dee saw his point. She also saw that his inspection of the car had been more thorough than it had appeared. In particular, when he spoke of new dents, he had concentrated on a large dent in the front fender. A body-sized dent? And the headlight beneath it had a spiderweb of cracks. What sort of accident had Carson had so recently? A hit-and-run?

Dee tried to put the thought out of her mind. But she slanted a sideways glance at Thatchpole, wondering if it had occurred to him, too.

"Anything new?" Carson was unaware of undercurrents. "What were you doing in the Admin Building, upsetting Giles? I saw him come rushing out just ahead of you."

"He was on his way to the hospital," Dee said. "He's meeting his family there. His father has regained consciousness."

"Has he?" Carson commented. "I wonder whether that's good or bad. Does it mean he's improving? Or is it a final rally just before the end?"

"I wouldn't know," Thatchpole said dourly. "But I can see why young Giles is dancing attendance on his doting Dad. You must do better in education than we do in manufacturing. I can't afford to give my offspring thousand-pound Swiss watches."

"You're joking!" Carson said. "Or else you need your eyes examined. Oops! . . . "

Carson swerved the car to avoid a couple of bicyclists who were coming towards him. As they had already begun evasive action when they saw who was driving, there was a near-miss. Undeterred, the cyclists waved at him cheerfully and pedalled past. It seemed that they were accustomed to Carson's erratic driving.

"You can let us off at the next corner." Thatchpole had gone pale.

"Are you sure?"

"We're not going far. We just got in to be sociable." Thatchpole was already grasping the door handle.

"And to invite you round to my hotel for a conference this evening," Dee said. "About seven."

"Council of war, eh?" Carson pulled over to the curb, scraping against it.

"We've just been talking to Professor Standfast. He sent for us—me—to let me know that he'd had a letter from one of the missing students. Martin Foster is back home in Canada—"

"And going to stay there." Thatchpole was looking better now that the car had stopped moving.

"That's another one accounted for, then." Carson was relieved, for a different reason. "It's still not beyond the realm of possibility that they'll all turn up safely yet."

"That's what Professor Standfast seemed to feel the letter proved," Dee said.

"And you don't?" Carson looked at her gravely. "No, you don't. All right, I'll see you this evening." He drove off.

Thatchpole flinched as the gears ground and brakes squealed. "How can any man be such a bad driver?"

"Absent-minded professor?" Dee suggested. And never so absent-minded as when behind the wheel of the car? Or could he be exaggerating his ineptness? Not very much, the state of the car showed that.

"This way." Thatchpole led her down a dog-leg turning she had not taken before. Ahead of them, a long low white wall with round porthole-like windows was set behind iron railings with a broad grassy strip in front of it on which sheep were grazing.

"I don't believe it!" Dee said. "In the middle of London!"

"Haven't you seen it before?" Thatchpole was mildly amused. "It's part of Coram's Fields. Pets Corner. They've got lots of other animals and birds. For the children."

"I haven't been this way before." Dee stared at the sheep, which continued grazing complacently. "Can we go in?"

"Against the rules. No adults allowed unless accompanied by a child. It's all to do with Captain Coram's legacy. This is the site of his original Foundling Hospital. It's still dedicated to the children of Central London. This is a great area for children. Great Ormond Street Children's Hospital is just over there—" He waved in the opposite direction.

"I know Connie's flat is in Coram's Mews—" They had turned another corner and so had the low white building. It was taller now and bordering the sidewalk, a door opening directly on to the pavement. Then the building ended and there were more iron railings, with gates behind which could be seen a long pool surrounded by all species of ducks, geese and wild fowl. Beyond it, the grounds opened out into a park containing a children's playground.

"It may be silly of me, but it never occurred to me that Coram had actually been someone's name."

"Oh yes, Captain Thomas Coram was one of the public benefactors of the eighteenth century. He was a sea captain who was so horrified by the abandoned children and dying babies he saw on his journeys between the docks and London that he fought for and managed to establish a Foundling Hospital in 1739.

"See here—" they paused before a massive stone column with a wide curved niche carved into it—"here's a bit of history. For a time this was where the foundlings were left. It's hollowed out, you see, so that the babes were protected from wind and rain. The poor little servant girl or other unfortunate left the baby here and rang the bell so that the gatekeeper could come and collect it while she hid somewhere across the street, watching to see that the child was safe and taking her last glimpse of it."

"How awful."

"Not at all. A much better alternative than the Workhouse—the babes didn't last long there. The mortality rate was two out of every three. It's always been a hard world, but this was a great improvement. A servant girl would have been dismissed, you know, for having an illegitimate baby and there'd be nowhere for her to go but on the streets. And a bastard wouldn't have been easy for any girl, of however good a family; money was tight, even in middle-class households, but mostly it was the shame she'd brought on herself and her family. Marriage chances gone, looked down on by her relatives, despised by her peers. Aye, and the child wouldn't have had an easy time of it, either. Best thing she could do was let it go.

"There's a Museum part to the Foundation on the other side of the Fields. You can see the pathetic little trinkets left with the babies as proof of identity. So many of the poor girls hoped they'd be able to reclaim their child some day; they clasped lockets round the babe's neck, tucked letters—those that could write—into the swaddling clothes, pinned cameos and brooches to the underthings. A lot of them held the dream that their luck would turn: they'd marry an understanding man, a relative would die and leave them enough to get by on . . . Who knows what they dreamed? But they hoped for a reunion one day—in this life, not the next."

"How heartbreaking." Dee's eyes were filled with tears for all the poor little wretches of a distant age.

"Aye, it was a brutal world. Nowadays—" his voice hardened— "they have a baby to jump the housing queue for a council flat and call themselves One-Parent Families. But—" he sighed—"I suppose it's better than this."

"Much better," Dee said firmly. "They can keep their babies and the stigma doesn't exist any more."

"Aye, but it's still a brutal world in other ways. New ways they never dreamed of." He looked off into the distance. "We can still lose our children, through no fault of our own. At least, we hope it isn't because of anything we've done—"

"Is Alison an only child?" Dee asked softly.

"No, I've got a son just about ready to join the company and begin working his way up to the Boardroom. And a married daughter who's in a fair way to making a grandfather of me any time now. But Alison is the baby. Her mother died two years ago."

"Oh, I'm sorry. I hadn't realized—"

"And you? Is Connie the only chick? And . . . are you a widow?"

"No-no. Hal Junior is younger than Connie, he's just started college. And Hal Senior is . . . at home. He . . . has other interests."

"The man's a fool!" Thatchpole did not pretend to misunderstand her. "He ought to be—"

"I think we should be getting along now," Dee said. "Coram's Mews isn't far."

"I don't think much of this place." Thatchpole stopped short at the entrance to the mews and frowned down it. "You say your girl lives *here*?"

"I didn't choose it for her," Dee said with some asperity. "She decided on it herself. I didn't know anything about it."

"I should think not!" He moved forward, shoulders hunched, as though prepared to fend off an attack. "Doesn't surprise me anyone wouldn't want to come back to this place."

"But they *would* return to their classes." Dee followed him down the mews. In the fading daylight of late afternoon, it was dark and shadowed. She was not surprised to see that the curtains were drawn over the windows of the flat. Like the mews itself, Tanya seemed to live in perpetual darkness.

"Here we are," Dee said, as Thatchpole walked past the doorway. "They're upstairs." She pushed at the door. As usual, it was open.

"That's not good." Thatchpole frowned and checked the latch. It worked. The door had been left unlocked deliberately. "No sense of self-preservation, these young ones. They think they're invulnerable. Silly little mugs."

"Excuse me—" The voice was thin and shrill, but it

made them jump. They turned to find that a small dark shape had detached itself from the shadows and crept up behind them.

"Excuse me," she said again. "But do you live here?"

"Who wants to know?" Thatchpole frowned, but could not hold on to the frown. Scarcely more than a child herself, she looked like one of the waifs who might have left her baby in the niche of the gatepost and run sobbing into the night. Except that her baby was still very much with her, distorting the otherwise slim form into a misshapen bulk.

"I do." The child quailed, but held her ground. "I'm looking for Eddie—and Jim. They own these garages. Have you seen them?"

"No," Dee said quietly, taking in the situation. "We haven't seen anyone. We don't live here, we've just come to visit someone."

"Here," Thatchpole said, as the girl swayed, "you'd better come upstairs and sit down." He had a sudden qualm. "Can you manage the stairs?"

"I can manage—" She lifted her head proudly and walked into the hallway. "But I don't think I'll go up." She sank down on one of the lower steps of the steep flight.

About eight months along, Dee reckoned, exchanging an anxious glance with Thatchpole. They did not urge her to try the stairs.

"That's it," Thatchpole said soothingly. "Just rest a bit. Can I get you anything?" It was a fairly meaningless offer, but well-meant. Presumably, he could have gone upstairs and begged a glass of water or cup of tea, but there was no guarantee that Tanya was at home.

"No, ta, I'm all right." She didn't look it; she looked strained and exhausted.

"How long have you been standing around in the mews?" Dee asked.

"Today? Just an hour or so. It's about the time he usually shows up—" She looked suddenly furtive and added quickly, "He works nights here. It's sort of an extra job, after he gets through at the market."

"But he hasn't been around lately," Thatchpole said. "And you're getting worried."

"I'm afraid he might be in trouble," she admitted. "He hasn't been at the market, either. And—and he didn't report to his Probation Officer, either." She began to cry.

"He owns these garages." Thatchpole glared at the wall as though he could see through it if he glared hard enough. "And your Connie—" he transferred the glare to Dee—"your Connie and her friends live in the flat over this garage. Did they rent the flat from him?"

"I don't know." Dee looked down at the weeping girl. "Did they?"

There was no response.

"Did your—" Thatchpole rephrased the question. "Did your . . . boyfriend—?"

She nodded vehemently without looking up.

"Did your boyfriend own the whole buildings or just the garage part of them?"

"What do you want to know for?" The girl looked up with a sudden flash of spirit. "Why are you asking all these questions? What are you—police?"

"Never!" Thatchpole said with enough emphasis to reassure her. "Look, this is Dee Sawyer and I'm Stan Thatchpole. What's your name?"

"Chrissie . . ." She was still wary, not giving them her last name,

"Well, Chrissie, we're trying to find a couple of people ourselves. If you can help us, you might be able to help yourself, too. That's why we're asking questions. All right?"

Warily, Chrissie nodded.

"Now, how much of these buildings did your boyfriend and his brother own?"

"Just the garages—they were expensive enough." She sniffed and dabbed at her eyes. "They've got them on ninety-nine-year leases. Ninety-six years, now."

"So the flat is on a separate lease," Thatchpole said. "Or else it still belongs to the freeholder. That's why it can be rented out. I wonder who the freeholder is."

"Don't know." Chrissie was recovering. "It was all done through Estate Agents. I never saw the leases."

"What do the leases matter?" Dee had a far more pertinent question. "When was the last time you saw your boyfriend?"

"Al—almost a month ago." The tears returned. "I can't believe it's been so long. We . . . we were talking about getting married. Before the baby came—" She broke into incoherent sobs.

So that was it. She thought he had run out on her.

"He wouldn't . . . do that . . . to me . . . " The words came brokenly. "He wouldn't." But he had—or so she feared.

"And his brother? Haven't you seen his brother, either?" Thatchpole spoke urgently. "Stop crying and answer me!"

"No—" Shocked out of her tears, she looked up at him fearfully. "They're both gone. They always did everything together—almost everything. Now they've gone off together. And Jim took Angie with him. She's my best friend. She's gone, too."

"Bloody hell!" Thatchpole said under his breath. "What's gone on here?"

"Where was Eddie the last time you saw him?" Dee was trying to find out.

"Up the market. Easter Saturday. It was the day of the big party, so he was awfully busy because he was running it—him and his friends. Making extra money, like." She was proud of his initiative.

"An Easter Party?" Dee asked.

"Sort of. The party was starting that Saturday night and going on through Sunday night right into Bank Holiday Monday. It was going to be great. But I had to tell him that I couldn't go, after all—" She looked down at her bulk. "I was feeling so sick. I wanted to go—honest—but I felt so awful. I was afraid I'd miscarry if I did."

"What *kind* of a party was it?" There was more intensity in Thatchpole's voice than the mere mention of an Easter Party, although it did seem to be an extraordinarily long one, would account for.

"A Warehouse Party. In Docklands." Chrissie slanted an upwards look at him. "They'd been planning it for ages with some friends. There's big money in those parties, you know."

"Aye, so I've heard," Thatchpole said grimly. "Especially in the drug-dealing that goes on on the side."

"Oh no!" Chrissie was instantly on the defensive. "Eddie wouldn't get mixed up in anything like that!"

"Then why has he got to report to a Probation Officer?" Thatchpole demanded brutally.

"Oh, that! That was just a bit of trouble about cars. Joy-riding, really. He was going to bring it back—honest."

Car thieves. The deserted mews, the dilapidated garages—carefully camouflaged to make them appear abandoned— suddenly began to make sense to Dee.

"What about bicycles?" She remembered the tangle of wheels and handlebars she had glimpsed through the cob-webbed garage window. "Did he do any joyriding on those, too?"

"How did you—?" Chrissie broke off and took refuge in tears again. "He never hurt anyone . . . just the insurance companies. People got their money . . . and got new cars . . ."

"And they brought the stolen cars here." Thatchpole was working it out. "Resprayed them, gave them new license numbers, then what? Shipped them over to the Continent? It's a big racket," he told Dee. "Cars are resold over there and it's almost impossible to trace them. They probably got rid of the bikes locally—inside this country, that is."

"Eddie never hurt anyone . . ." Chrissie was still defending the father of her child. "There's never been any violence. Not before—That's why I'm scared." The sobs shook her so that she was almost incoherent. "He didn't know . . . I saw . . . the gun . . . that day."

"What gun?" Thatchpole thundered.

"He . . . he had a gun. A *real* gun . . . not one of those little bitty things . . ." For a moment, pride shaded her voice. "One of those Army ones that go on shooting. A Kali-something . . ."

"Good Christ!" Thatchpole said. "A submachine-gun! How did he get his hands on that?"

"He knows people . . . he has friends. You can get anything . . . if you have friends."

"Some friends!" Thatchpole said. "Why did he want such a gun?"

"I think . . . he was . . . expecting trouble . . ."

Dee leaned against the wall, feeling sick. She tried to convince herself that this had nothing to do with Connie. But . . . Tanya had bought a "guard dog" . . . Tanya had been expecting trouble, too. Where *was* Tanya? With all this noise in the lower hall, surely she would have opened the door if she were home.

"That's it!" Thatchpole said. "This time the police will have to take notice!"

"Have you any reason to suspect foul play?" the police had asked. Yes, they probably would pay attention now.

"No!" Chrissie lunged to her feet, screaming. "No! Don't go near the police! You'll get Eddie into terrible trouble—"

"I'd say he was already in terrible trouble." Thatchpole was grim. "The police—"

"No! No! They—They—" The tenor of her screams changed. She bent double, clutching herself.

"Christ!" Thatchpole leaped back. "She's not having it here!"

"I don't think so." Dee stepped forward and put her arms around the girl. "I think it's just hysteria—but this isn't doing her any good. We ought to get her to a hospital. Just to be sure."

"Hang on." Thatchpole spoke urgently to both of them. "I'll go and get a taxi. Just hang on!"

CHAPTER 26

Cora loved the restaurant. The fragrant smells and bustle of the kitchen—yes, even the florid Italian cursing—the friendly patrons in the dining-room, the other waitresses who were never too busy to nudge her and whisper a warning when she was about to make some mistake. Oh yes, this was going to be a great place to work on weekends.

She would enjoy it even more when she wasn't so tired. Next Friday she would go back to her room and lie down and rest for a couple of hours between finishing at the sandwich shop and starting here. That long walk with André had been almost too much for her, but she hadn't wanted to discourage him. He'd been so eager to take the first steps towards friendship—and so had she. They were also the first steps towards normalcy and a new life. The world might not quite be her oyster yet—but it was looking a lot less terrifying than it had when she had first become aware of it as the mental fog began to lift.

In a way, though, it was good to be too tired to think. Not that she had been doing much thinking, anyway. Take one day at a time and don't worry about the future—or the past—that was the way to live. It also helped to keep busy and work among busy people—far too busy to think about you or ask questions. Although André might become a problem as they got to know each other better. But worry about that when it happens.

A new party had come in, four people without reservations. Tourists who had scanned the menu posted outside and found it to their liking. Rosa led them to a table at the back and signalled to Cora to come and attend them.

They were breaking her in on the customers who didn't matter, the casuals, here for the first and possibly only time. Passing trade. It was fair enough. Later, when she was better trained, they would let her wait on the valued patrons. And the one-timers would never know the difference, probably they expected a waitress to be awkward, anyway.

"Good evening." She dealt out the menus expertly, still feeling a bit inhospitable not to be bringing everyone a glass of water. But she had been laughed out of that on her first attempt. ("In this restaurant, they drink wine," Rosa had said, shaking her head at Cora's eccentricity.) Cora set the wine list down at the elder gentleman's elbow, although most people, after studying it earnestly, wound up ordering the House Red or House White. They liked to look at the options, though.

These were the usual group who had been strolling along the front, then exploring the antiques shops in The Lanes, out for a good time and having it. They spoke with Northern accents and kept comparing Brighton to some place called Cleethorpes. They found the comparison hilarious.

Cora retreated quietly to wait until they were ready to order. She was learning the signs and it was going to take them a while; they had evidently stopped in at a couple of pubs first.

She jotted down the number of their table on her order pad, in readiness for the moment they called her over, and looked around, checking her other tables. There were only two. At one, they were lingering so long over coffee that they might still be here when the place closed. At the other, they had stopped eating and were in intense discussion, perhaps quarrelling; it didn't look as though they'd be ordering dessert.

Finally, the new table beckoned to her and she went back to them. Now they were in a hurry. She scribbled down their orders.

"And hurry up with that minestrone—" one of them called after her jovially as she moved towards the kitchen. "We're starving!"

She waved acknowledgement and let the kitchen door swing shut behind her. For an anxious moment, as the chef waited patiently, she was afraid she was not going to be able to read her own writing. There was no problem about the minestrone, but there was something else scribbled above it. She turned the order pad to the left and then to the right, trying to decipher it—

Dear Mom—

She dropped the order pad and swayed.

"Cora, are you all right?" Rosa rushed forward to steady her. "You gonna faint?"

"No. No, I'm all right." She shook herself and stooped to retrieve the order pad.

"You're overdoing it. You're not used to carrying all those heavy dishes around. You got to work your way into it, get your muscles toned up. Here—" Rosa reached for the tray with the four bowls of minestrone on it. "I'll take this in to them. You sit down and rest for a minute."

"I'll be all right," Cora said faintly, still clutching the pad as though she would never let go of it. Perhaps she wouldn't. It no longer belonged to the restaurant—it be-

longed to her. It held a message to herself from herself—
her buried self.

Spirit writing, something told her it was called. Or *automatic writing*. In her exhausted state, she had doodled
unwittingly on the pad, not even thinking about it, while
waiting for the customers to call her over to give her their
orders. If they had taken just a little longer over their decisions, what else would she have written?

"You gonna be all right?" Mr. Pacelli's uncle, also Mr.
Pacelli, came over to frown down at her. "Why don't you
go home now? Rosa can take over your tables. It's almost
closing time, anyway."

"I can manage." Cora forced a smile, hoping he would
insist. She was frantic to get home now. To sit alone in the
dark with pen and paper—and discover what else she
might write.

"Don't worry, I'm not sacking you." His smile was unforced. "First time is always rough—you've lasted longer
than a lot of them. Look, take tomorrow off—it's only a
family wedding. They'll be in and out of the kitchen helping themselves most of the time anyway. Come back
Sunday."

"Well . . . if you don't mind . . . "

"Run along. Rosa will sort out your tips with you on
Sunday." He counted out some money and pressed it into
her hand. "Just don't tell Giorgio I ran you right down
into the ground, huh? He likes you; he'll kill me."

Involuntarily, she flinched.

"Hey, hey, I'm only joking! We're not Mafia, you
know. You sure you're gonna be OK? You want Rosa to
go home with you?"

"No, no, thanks. I'm OK." She could hardly wait to get
away now. She headed for the back to change out of her

uniform. She hoped he didn't notice that she still held the order pad. She had to get out of here before he asked for that back. Rosa could sort out the orders with the customers.

But back in her room, after two hours of struggling, she had to admit defeat. Perhaps she wasn't relaxed enough—how could she be? Or maybe she'd passed the exact point in exhaustion that allowed it to happen. But it wasn't working.

The hand holding the pen refused to move. Over and over again, she had written: *Dear Mom*—But the hand had stubbornly refused to add anything to that fragment of information.

She was too excited, had hoped for too much. The adrenalin was flowing—but that was all. The knowledge was still locked away in some recess of her shuttered mind.

She had learned only one thing: there was a *Mom*, a *Dear Mom*, out there somewhere. Or . . . there had been.

She knew something else about amnesia; the fact had surfaced suddenly, in the way most of her inner revelations did. She knew that some people developed amnesia when their world had become too appalling to cope with. Traumatic amnesia. They retreated into the merciful blankness rather than face a reality which had become too painful to bear.

London . . . London was the most painful thought she had ever had in this new untarnished life. Did that mean that the answer was there?

Should she—*could* she—go to London . . . go *back* to London . . . and see if the answer was waiting for her there?

CHAPTER 27

Heidi and Tanya arrived together.

Dee had not realized how much she had been worrying about Tanya until she opened the door and saw her.

"Thank goodness!" she said. "You got my note." That scrap of paper, hastily scribbled on and thrust under the door while Thatchpole bundled Chrissie into the taxi.

"Of course." Tanya raised her eyebrows, surprised at Dee's vehemence. "Steady, Barney—" The pup was leaping forward to paw at Dee, his old friend, gurgling with delight.

"I got your message, too." Heidi obviously felt a bit left out. "What's up?"

What, indeed? Dee smiled, hoping Thatchpole would take the initiative on that question. The time spent getting Chrissie settled into the Maternity Ward had left her almost too spent to talk. They had arrived back here barely in time to greet their guests.

"Ooh-uuh!" Heidi's indrawn breath as she stepped into the room reminded Dee that she was still wearing Connie's clothes. There was no reaction from Tanya, but then, the outfit had been packed into the suitcase left with Heidi. How much more prying had Heidi actually done?

"Tea or coffee?" Thatchpole invited firmly. He and Dee had already had something stronger to brace them for the evening ahead. After Chrissie, they had needed it.

"Tea, please." Tanya moved straight towards the buffet

spread. "And could I have a saucer of milk for Barney, please? His meals have been a bit skimpy today and I know he'd like some. He's still a puppy."

"Milk for Barney." Thatchpole solemnly filled that order first and set the saucer of milk on the floor. Barney dived into it enthusiastically. "That's a fine pup you have there. What is he?"

"A Basenji." Tanya looked down with pride. "He's shaping up beautifully. I may show him yet."

"A Crufts winner if I ever saw one," Thatchpole agreed. He poured tea for Tanya and they retreated to a corner, still talking dogs. Dee had never seen Tanya so animated—was it because of the doggy conversation, or Thatchpole?

Another knock at the door heralded Dr. Carson. The party was getting into full swing.

"Tea or coffee?" Dee suggested, following Thatchpole's lead.

"Is that the best on offer?" Carson called her bluff. "I don't know about you, but I've had a hard day."

He looked it. Dee glanced at the others: Heidi had helped herself to coffee and a sandwich and was crouched beside Barney, sharing the sandwich with him. Tanya was still fully occupied with Thatchpole.

"Good girl!" Carson said, as she opened the cabinet beneath the buffet and gestured towards the private stock. "I'll have a Scotch."

"With or without ice?"

"As a tribute to your country, I'll have ice—so long as you don't overdo it." He accepted the drink with satisfaction. "That's what I like about Americans—they have loose wrists."

Dee gathered that she had poured double, or perhaps

treble, the usual pub measure—yet it was a normal American measure.

"Are we all here?" Carson looked around.

"All except Giles Abbott. He had to visit his father in hospital; he said he might be late."

"Oh yes." Carson looked bemused. "Actually, I wouldn't count on Giles. There's been fresh word from the hospital. His father has worsened again. The family are staying by the bedside."

"Oh, poor Giles!" Again, Dee felt the poignant twinge; half sympathy, half envy. The Abbott family knew what was happening to their dear one.

"You'd best have something stronger yourself." Carson poured the Scotch as generously as she had. "And get stuck into those sandwiches. You need to keep up your strength."

"Yes . . . " She picked up one blindly. They were all alike, the filling so thin it was hard to believe they weren't just bread-and-butter stuck together. There wasn't much strength to be found in them.

Thin as it was, the filling was also sloppy and some of it dribbled out as she bit into it. This being England, the hotel hadn't bothered to supply paper napkins and Thatchpole hadn't thought to include them in his instructions. She fumbled in her jacket pocket for the paper handkerchief she had placed there earlier. As she pulled it out, something fell to the floor.

She and Carson stooped for it at the same time, but she was faster. It was just a circle of yellow paper with a sticky back, two large dots and a semi-circle on the yellow surface. She looked at it with disappointment. It had been something belonging to Connie and for one wild instant she had hoped it might be a clue, but it was just a Smiley sticker.

"What's that?" Thatchpole hadn't missed a thing. He was beside her now, taking the silly scrap from her. "Where did you get this?"

"It was in the pocket. It must belong to Connie. This is her jacket."

"Oh Christ!" Thatchpole had gone pale, he looked at her in consternation.

"It's only a Smiley sticker," Dee said. He was acting as though she had found something to do with witchcraft. "We have them in the States, too. It's nothing."

"Oh, gee, Mrs. Sawyer—" Heidi looked desperately unhappy. "They don't mean the same thing at all over here."

"What do they mean over here?" Dee looked from Heidi's face to Thatchpole's and suspected that she did not really want to know the answer.

"Well, they're sort of . . ." Heidi trailed off, searching for the right words. "Sort of a signal to other people that you're interested in the same things. The same kind of music and—"

"Acid House!" Thatchpole broke in sharply. "Acid Rock! Wild Parties! Drugs!"

"No!" Dee said. "Not Connie!"

"It doesn't have to mean drugs," Heidi said quickly. "Lots of kids just go for the music and the company. Hundreds and hundreds go to those parties. Sometimes thousands. They don't all do drugs."

"But the drugs are there." Thatchpole glared at her. "So are the dealers and pushers. Those kinds of parties are impossible to police."

"Shit, the police don't get anywhere near them!

Nobody knows where they're going to be held until the last minute. The buzz just goes round that there's going to be one at Easter, or whenever, and you get a telephone number to call a couple of hours before on the day. Then everybody converges on the spot—"

"You seem to know a lot about it, young woman!" Thatchpole glared at her.

"Oh, um, everybody does—" Heidi looked for support. "You can't help know around a school. I'll bet even Dr. Carson knows."

"She's right," Carson said. "Anyone around a college or university can't help knowing. We may not approve, but it's impossible to stop these things. We can only hope that the venue is far enough away to reduce the nuisance to us. In the summer, they tend to be held in fields way out in the country. When the weather is bad, the organizers take over anything with a roof and plenty of room. They started out in abandoned warehouses, but they've been held in places like old airplane hangars, unused film studios, deserted mansions—"

"Warehouses!" Thatchpole said softly.

"Yeah," Heidi said. "Sometimes they're called Warehouse Parties. Mostly, though, it's Acid House Parties—anyway, that's what the media keep calling them, although the kids have another name for them now—"

"Warehouse Party," Dee whispered, meeting Thatchpole's eyes. "That girl said . . ." She could not go on. A big Easter weekend party in a warehouse, run by a couple of youths on Probation who had acquired a submachine-gun because they were expecting trouble . . .

"Connie!" Dee whispered again, closing her eyes in anguish. "Oh, Connie . . ."

"Look, it's not the end of the world if she *did* go to an

Acid House Party." Heidi defended her friend. "She wouldn't do anything stupid."

"Then where is she?" Thatchpole demanded. "And where's my Alison? They went to the party together, didn't they?"

"Well, gee, I guess so. Connie wanted me to go, but I'd already booked an Easter tour to Switzerland. Between Switzerland and Docklands, there was no contest!" She grinned briefly before remembering that it was no laughing matter. "I'm sorry."

"Docklands . . ." Thatchpole said slowly. "There are still miles of undeveloped areas along the river, old wharves, crumbling warehouses. Not as many as there used to be, but the developers hadn't got round to all of them before the slump slowed everything down." He moved towards the door, Dee following him.

"There's no guarantee that the girls are anywhere near there." Carson tried to make them see sense. "Quite the contrary. Anything that happens at one of those parties is spread all over the front pages and the television screens the next day. The party must have gone off all right. There won't be anything to find. I mean—"

"We know what you mean," Thatchpole said. "But it's the only lead we've got."

"But you can't just jump into your car and go driving wildly all over Docklands." Carson didn't sound too convincing; he knew that they could.

But he didn't know about Chrissie and they weren't about to tell him now. Dee met Thatchpole's eyes in silent agreement. They would go back to the Maternity Ward and hope that Chrissie could give them more specific directions for finding the right warehouse.

"Why don't we all go?" Heidi was game for adventure;

it was one of the reasons she and Connie had become such good friends.

"I don't think I can." Tanya had been very quiet, now she jangled the puppy's leash, using him as an excuse. "Barney—I have to take Barney home. He's getting over-tired. He's still a puppy."

Thatchpole ignored both girls. Dee noticed that Carson had not volunteered to come along. Convinced that this would be a wild goose chase, he wanted no part of it.

The knock on the door startled them all. Thatchpole was nearest, he opened it and stepped back.

"I'm sorry I'm late." Giles walked unseeingly into the room. "I was . . . delayed."

"Giles." Carson came forward. "Is everything all right?"

"Are you OK, Giles?" Heidi asked concernedly. "You don't look so hot."

"Oh yes." Giles gave them both a travesty of a smile. "*I'm* all right."

"Come and sit down." Carson led him to a chair.

"I don't like the look of this," Thatchpole muttered under his breath to Dee. "Let's hold on a bit. I'll ring the hospital instead. If the lass won't answer my questions over the phone, *then* we'll go over and browbeat her in person."

Dee nodded and went to get Giles a drink. He looked as though he needed one, a stiff one.

Carson was already at the cabinet, bringing out the Scotch. He met Dee's eyes and shook his head. "What do you think we ought to do with him?" he asked.

"You know him better than I do," Dee said. "*You* decide."

Heidi and Tanya had advanced to stand beside Giles's

chair, but only Barney seemed able to reach him. Barney pawed at Giles's knee and Giles patted him absently.

"Here." Carson thrust the glass at him.

"Thanks." Giles drank half of it at a gulp and didn't seem to notice that no water had been added.

"For God's sake, Giles—" Heidi rushed in where the others feared to tread. "What's the matter with you?"

"I'm all—"

"The hell you are! Even Barney can see you're a wreck! What's happened?"

In the background, Thatchpole had dialed the hospital where they had left Chrissie and was speaking softly into the phone.

"You've just come from the hospital—" Dee prompted gently.

"Yes . . ." Unconsciously, Giles gave a deep sigh. "Hospital . . . yes."

"I was talking to Standfast about an hour ago," Carson said delicately. "He said something about a relapse . . ."

"Relapse!" Giles uttered a short mirthless bark, probably intended to be a sardonic laugh. Barney whined in sympathy. "I suppose you could call it a relapse. He's dead!"

"Oh, I'm sorry—"

"Shit, Giles!"

"How rotten, Giles. I'm most terribly sorry." Tanya pulled at Barney trying to draw him away. "Don't bother Giles now," she told the puppy.

"He's not bothering me." Giles bent over the puppy; it was a way of keeping his face averted.

"You want to talk about it?" Heidi offered. "It's supposed to help, you know."

"Help!" The strangulated voice seemed to belong to

someone else, someone who was perhaps actually calling for help. "He's dead. There's nothing anyone can do."

Nothing . . . Dee heard the echo of Mrs. Daniels.

"But I thought he was recovering." Dee said it only to prod him to keep on talking. It *would* help him, whether he believed it or not. "When we spoke to you earlier, you were on the way to the hospital because he had recovered consciousness."

"Earlier . . . " Giles raised his head and gazed out into a wasteland where time had become meaningless. "Yes, I was going to meet my family there. My mother was so encouraged—"

"It's tough," Heidi said. She glanced at Dee in an almost frightened way, as though she had suddenly recollected that it was tough for Dee, too.

"They were all there when I got there." Now that he had begun to tell them, Giles continued compulsively. "My mother had already been in to see him. He'd even spoken to her, but she couldn't understand what he was saying because he wasn't articulating clearly enough. She thought he said my name. He wanted to see me. My sisters, too, of course, but—but I'm his only son.

"We—We all went in together. Maybe we shouldn't have. Maybe there were too many of us, it was too much for him. But the nurse wasn't around, so we couldn't ask. We all went in—"

"I don't think it would have made any difference at that stage." Carson tried to comfort him.

"Yes . . . no . . ." Giles shrugged. "Anyway, we did it. My father was sitting up in bed and looking fairly well, considering. He looked at my mother, my sisters, me . . . I think he tried to smile, but the way his mouth was dragged down on one side—Then he went a funny color and started to choke. Then he—he just died. Just like that." Giles bent over Barney again, hiding his face.

In the uncomfortable silence, Dee looked away from Giles in his misery and saw Thatchpole signalling to her from the telephone. He had completed his call and his face was thunderous.

"What is it?" Dee moved back to join him. "What did she say?"

"She isn't there. The little fool signed herself out just after we left. She's gone home—wherever that is!"

"Doesn't the hospital have an address on her records?"

"You don't imagine she told them the truth?"

No, Dee hadn't imagined that for a moment. She had seen the sly look in Chrissie's eyes as she glibly rattled off her supposed address. Wherever Chrissie lived, it was not there.

"She'll come back to the mews. It's the only place she knows, apart from the market, where her Eddie might show up again."

"Aye, but will we see her? She'll be twice as fly now."

"We'll ask Tanya to keep a lookout—" But Tanya stayed behind closed curtains, perhaps because she had felt herself observed, sensed a watching presence in the mews. If they explained to her that the watcher was only a young pregnant girl, scarcely less frightened than herself, would Tanya be braver?

Thatchpole gave a noncommittal grunt, possibly following her thoughts, or perhaps having doubts of his own.

"We can try—" Dee started back towards the group hovering uncertainly around Giles. True to form, Tanya had moved away from them, distancing herself slightly, although allowing Barney to remain nuzzling Giles's face and providing the only tactile comfort available.

The telephone rang, halting Dee in her tracks. She turned to see Thatchpole automatically lifting the receiver.

"Yes, what is it?" he barked into the mouthpiece, obviously transported back to his own office by the unexpected summons.

"Who—? What—? Oh—" Slightly shamefaced, he handed the receiver to Dee. "It's for you."

"Hello? *Who* is it—?" For a moment, she could not understand the garbled voice at the other end of the line. "Oh! Oh, Hal . . . "

"Yes, Hal!" And Hal was furious. "Who was that? Who answered your phone?"

"How nice of you to get around to calling, Hal," she said coldly. "I know how busy you are. But I'm afraid there's no news about Connie yet. She's still missing and I'm still trying to find her."

"Oh yes, sure, I'm worried about Connie—" Caught wrong-footed, he tried to bluster. "But I asked you—"

"Yes, dear, and I might have a few things to ask *you* about before too long."

"Oh!" He deflated. "It *was* you on the phone. Listen, I can explain—"

"And I'll be fascinated to hear your explanation. It was about four o'clock in the morning, wasn't it?"

"The man's a fool!" Thatchpole growled loudly.

"Who *is* that?" Hal had heard and it set him off again. "What's going on there? Dee, do you have a man in your room?"

"As a matter of fact—" Dee smiled as sweetly as though Hal could see her, revelling in a moment of pure enjoyment.

"To tell the absolute truth, Hal, I have *three* men in my room."

She replaced the receiver quietly.

CHAPTER 28

It had been a long time since he had slept the night through. Perhaps he might never again.

Was it worth it? Too late to think about that. Too many other things to think about, more pressing problems. Nothing but problems these days.

Disbelief still tinged his every thought when he let himself go, let himself think about it. He'd been doing so well, so well. His new career had been building nicely, success within his grasp . . .

Building . . . buildings . . . What was happening down among the cranes and bulldozers? Dare he go down there and look?

No, no, better to keep away. Don't draw any attention to the area. Not even accidentally. You never can tell who might be watching. Too many people crowding around now . . . too curious . . .

Dee Sawyer! Damn her! Damn the bitch for whelping Connie! Where was Connie? Even her mother couldn't find her. He'd pinned most of his hope on Dee Sawyer's leading him to Connie.

Was he so sure that Connie wasn't dead? He wasn't sure of anything. Not any more.

It was possible. Possible she had collapsed and died

after staggering free of the warehouse. More than possible that some vagrant had come along, helped himself to the cashmere coat and all the cash in the pockets, then rolled the body into the river.

The Thames is a tidal river, deep and swift, carrying all the flotsam and jetsam dumped into it out to sea every time the tide turns. Bodies, too.

In that case, there was no chance of getting the money back. But there was still plenty left. Perhaps he should just cut and run.

But . . . leave everything behind? Worse, draw attention to himself? He was not suspected—he was above suspicion—right now. Why do anything to change that? Stay here, keep your head down, brazen it out.

Nothing might ever happen. Not for years. If then. Construction companies went broke all the time. Why shouldn't it happen before they reached the . . . the building to be demolished? It could be years before someone else went to work on the site. If enough time had passed, the trail would be so cold that it would never lead to him.

They couldn't get him now . . . without witnesses.

It was looking increasingly unlikely that dear Constance was willing—or able—to come forward with any accusations. But what about the one who had fled back to Canada? It was a good sign that Martin Foster had had sense enough to leave the country. It meant that he didn't want to get involved. Or was too terrified to. Either way, he was beyond reach at the moment. Let him go. If he showed signs of giving trouble in the future . . . Well, time enough to worry about that when it happened.

Happened . . . his mind twisted back on itself again, going round and round on the same endless track. *How*

*had it all happened? How had it all exploded in his face
so suddenly?*

No, don't think about that! Wipe it out. You'll never get
to sleep if you start that again. You need your sleep.
You've got to get up in the morning . . . face the world . . .
make decisions . . .

Decisions—oh God!

He turned over again, thumped the pillow again, tried
to control his thoughts again. Again and again and
again—was the rest of his life to be like this?

Worse, if they caught him. Disgrace. Prison. An end to
all hopes and ambitions. Better to live with an unquiet
conscience every night than to live with that.

Live—oh God! He was alive and they were dead. And
the bulldozers were creeping closer.

Suppose they had already been found? The police kept
the lid on things more often than the public suspected.
You only discovered it when the story eventually broke
and you realized that the child had been kidnapped three
weeks ago and the police had been monitoring the case,
but keeping all information from the media until the child
had been safely returned. And look at the way they staked
out drug operations for weeks and months, without a word
being whispered—until after they had swooped and made
their arrests.

Were they secretly watching his every movement even
now? Were they following him, bugging his phone, writing their reports and waiting for their moment to swoop?

No, they couldn't be. That sort of treatment was reserved for professional criminals involved in major
crimes. He wasn't a criminal, not a real one. His was more
the accidental, almost-domestic violence. He wasn't a repeat offender. No, don't think about Henry.

If they knew about him, they'd have been at the door long ago and he'd be sleeping in a cell right now.

Sleeping . . . he couldn't go on like this. He had to get some rest. He'd have to see about getting some sleeping pills. That shouldn't be hard.

CHAPTER 29

For the first time since she had arrived, Dee slept late in the morning. She couldn't believe it when she looked at the clock and saw that it was quarter to eleven.

It was not just the jetlag, she forgave herself, it had also turned into an unexpectedly late night last night.

Carson, thank heavens, had taken responsibility for Giles Abbott and had carried him off for more drinks and what sympathy could be offered before delivering him home to his family.

Tanya, claiming responsibility for Barney, had removed herself and the puppy as soon as the party had shown signs of breaking up.

Heidi had made a polite feint towards leaving, but had not been able to disguise her relief when Thatchpole insisted that she join himself and Dee for a "proper" meal. It had not been until later that Heidi had discovered that she was about to sing for her supper—and for how long and on such a sustained note.

Before a late supper at Boulestin's, Thatchpole had persuaded Heidi (she almost thought it was her own idea) to lead them on a tour of the venues where her coevals queued for blocks in order to gain admittance to the trendy clubs where the latest gods of what passed for music were performing that night.

It was a forlorn hope, a vain hope—even Thatchpole in his secret heart must have known that—but it *was* a hope and it had to be given its chance, even though it finally left them feeling more hopeless than ever.

They trailed her down the Charing Cross Road, over into one of the narrow turnings leading to the Embankment, even along to the end of Piccadilly where would-be customers waited for admittance to the Hard Rock Café. Everywhere there were hordes of youngsters queuing for blocks. So many of them, so very many more than she had imagined there could be.

She had felt the tremor of Thatchpole's hand grasping her arm and knew that he felt the same way. Even if Connie and Alison were in one of those queues, how could they pick them out? A turned head, a step sideways, and the girl would have vanished into the mass even as they passed.

Only Heidi had radiated hope and confidence as they searched each queue. "Not here," she had decided cheerfully, while Dee and Thatchpole were still straining their eyes, trying to penetrate the obscuring make-up, the trendy hairstyles. "Let's try the next place."

There had been so many places, so many queues, so many hundreds—perhaps thousands—of kids. But no Connie. No Alison.

"And these are just the ones standing outside," Thatchpole said glumly. "We don't know how many hundreds more are already inside these places."

"It's like this all weekend—" Heidi had failed to realize that she was not cheering them on. "We can try again tomorrow night. There are dozens of gigs going on all over London."

London, Dee recollected dismally, comprised some twenty-five square miles. Heidi sounded as though she were familiar with every one of them and—with a taxi at her command—ready to investigate every one of them.

"That's it!" Thatchpole lowered his flag just as Dee's legs threatened to fold up under her. "That's enough. We can't spend all night on obbo. Let's go and eat!"

"*What* did you say?" Both Heidi and Dee whirled on him.

"Let's go and eat," he repeated blankly. "What's the matter?"

"Before that—" Dee stared at him. "That word you used—"

"Obbo?" He was defensive. "I wasn't swearing, it's slang. Short for observation."

"Then Mass Obbo—" Heidi was triumphant. "That would mean Mass Observation, right?"

"That's right. Something to do with sociology—there was a lot of it during the war. Ordinary people worked for it, keeping day-to-day accounts of their lives. The idea was, put them all together and you got a pattern of society and what was really happening to it. I think it's still going on in a minor way. Why? What's this all about?"

"Connie mentioned it in her diary," Dee said. "I think she was going to try her hand at it."

Why not me? Had Connie been observing too much in that sinister mews? Was there another diary or notebook in which she had been writing it all down: the day-to-day doings of the friendly local car thieves in the mews beneath her windows? If they'd caught her at it—

Dee shuddered. Connie, just before she left home, had

been thinking about her future career, testing the idea of becoming an investigative reporter. It was Hal who had pointed out that some of them had short careers—because they had short lives. You had to be very careful about the people and things you were investigating.

And the car thieves had disappeared, too, after . . . after what? Had they discovered what Connie was doing, carried out a grim reprisal, then gone on the run? Jaycee and Maggie had also lived in the mews flat and they had disappeared, too. Had they been included in some revenge attack?

But Tanya lived there, too, and she was still all right. Tanya and the barkless puppy with milk teeth she was depending upon to protect her. Had she escaped because she had been away buying the puppy that weekend? How ironic if that half-helpless little creature had saved her life, after all.

"Steady on." Thatchpole touched her shoulder and gave it a gentle squeeze.

"Yes . . ." Dee realized that she had been shuddering. She wanted to tell him what she had been thinking—but not in front of Heidi.

"We've all had enough tonight. Let's go and eat."

"You're sure?" Heidi sounded disappointed. "We haven't even been to the pubs at World's End yet."

Dee had shuddered again. World's End had sounded entirely too apt.

Now Dee lifted the telephone to check the time with the switchboard, just to make sure that her own clock had not gone berserk.

"Ten-forty-nine," the switchboard assured her cheerfully. "You've had two calls from the States, but your friend, Mr. Thatchpole, told us you weren't to be disturbed for any reason. They left their number—" She read off the familiar number.

"Thank you." Dee deduced that her friend, Mr. Thatchpole, had tipped liberally to ensure her privacy. "I'll get in touch with them later."

Would she? Hal would be furious, of course, and the last thing she needed was an ill-tempered tirade from someone who didn't care enough to be here when she needed him. Let him wait; she'd done enough waiting in the past couple of years.

The phone rang almost as soon as she had replaced the receiver. Hal, trying again? She couldn't avoid answering it, the switchboard operator knew she was up and awake now.

"Hello—? Oh, Stan." She needn't have worried. Whether or not Hal tried again, switchboard was going to give precedence to the extravagantly-tipping Mr. Thatchpole. "I just got up."

"I know. I made arrangements to be informed as soon as you began stirring."

"Did you?" It must have been a fantastic tip.

"I was worried. You were in a bit of a state last night. Scarcely to be wondered at, but I wanted to make sure you were all right this morning. Did you get any sleep at all?"

"Some. Off and on . . . between nightmares. And you?"

"Nightmares, too." He sighed. "Only natural, I suppose, but it's exhausting." He sounded tired, spent. "You ready for another day of it?"

"As ready as you are. Stan . . ." She hesitated, unsure of his reaction to what she was about to propose.

"What?" He sounded more alert.

"Stan, what you said yesterday—in Standfast's office—about hiring a private detective. Did you mean it? I . . . I think it might be a good idea to get a professional in on this. Since the police won't help us."

"They might help us now—with what we've been finding out. But there might be a lot of time wasted while they got the machinery into gear. A detective, mm, I was just trying to put the wind up Standfast, but it might be a last resort."

"What other options do we have left?" She hoped she didn't sound quite as discouraged as she felt.

"Not many, that's a fact." He sighed again. "I thought it wouldn't be so difficult—once I was on the spot."

"That's what I thought, too, but it isn't working out that way. We need more help than we've been getting. Heidi and the others mean well, but they don't know enough to—"

"You're right," he agreed. "We've given it our best shot— and we can keep on working at it—but it can't hurt to call in a private inquiry agent. Most of the ones I've had any dealings with have specialized in industrial espionage, but I'll see if they can recommend anyone more suited to our needs."

"I'd like to get someone today."

"So would I, luv, but it's Saturday. You want to be realistic about this. Monday morning is probably going to be the best we can do."

"Monday . . ." Dee echoed. "It seems so far away." She felt that she was caught in a time warp, the days of the week had lost all meaning. She had actually forgotten that offices closed for the weekend and people went away. Presumably, even private detectives, unless they were on an urgent case, took Saturday and Sunday off— or at least went over their findings and wrote up their reports at home.

"You're heading for a nervous breakdown if you don't let up a bit," Thatchpole said.

"I can't!" She felt her muscles tense. "Not while Connie—"

"You'll be no use to her if you're a basket case! I'm just as worried about Alison, but we've got to be sensible. In fact, maybe we can kill two birds with one—I'm sorry, I didn't mean that the way it came out. I mean, I've been thinking, remembering . . . when all the children were small, my wife and I used to take them to Brighton for their holidays. Alison loved it there.

"You pointed out that they could be anywhere in the country. Well, if they're not in London, I'd stake something on Brighton. It looks as though, at best, something happened to thoroughly upset and frighten them—"

"Yes," Dee said. He didn't say what might have happened at worst. He didn't have to.

"If those silly little fools got themselves in too deep with car thieves and wild parties, they might have run away. Alison would want to go somewhere she already knew, where she'd felt safe and happy. She'd have persuaded Connie that Brighton was a good place to, well, to retreat to. Until the trouble blew over."

Hide was the word he didn't want to say.

"You may be right," Dee said cautiously. He knew his daughter; if he said that was where Alison would run, then she would. And Connie would go along, because she was Alison's friend, and because she didn't know any other hiding places in this country.

"Why don't we drive down and look around? It can't do any harm."

"Today?" Dee heard her voice rise in consternation. "But Heidi is going to take us to more venues—It's too far—"

"It's not and Heidi can come with us. She must have heard of clubs down there and three pairs of eyes will be more useful than two."

"But . . ." Dee could not explain her sudden curious reluctance to leave London.

"We'll have lunch and talk it over. I'll collect Heidi and pick you up in an hour."

CHAPTER 30

It was a glorious day, a day to make the heart sing and the spirit soar. The sun was bright, the sea sparkling, the air could almost lift you up and carry you across the Channel. It was an inspirational day, a day for legendary deeds, for setting off for the Crusades, for slaying dragons, for sailing to the Spanish Main, for searching for the Holy Grail . . .

For going up to London . . . ?

Cora glanced sideways at André, who had insisted on buying the tickets. He had been waiting outside the house for her this morning, bubbling over with enthusiasm for his great idea.

"Saturday! No language class. No sandwich shop. We go to London! You show me the looks—"

"The sights," she said automatically, falling into the trap.

"Sights!" He chortled with glee. "You see how bad I need my interpreter, my friend?"

"I think your English is a lot better than you pretend it is," she said severely, but spoiled it by smiling.

"No! No! I am so stupid. You must come or I get lost."

Lost . . . She stopped smiling. How long could she go on being lost to the world, now that she knew there was a world out there? *Dear Mom* . . .

"Please—" He was watching her anxiously, afraid that he had offended her in some way because she had stopped smiling. "You come with me?"

"Why not?" She waited for the answer to surface from within herself, but nothing happened. London no longer seemed so frightening, so repellent. Was it because she would have André with her?

"Good!" He caught her hand. "Hurry and we take the next train!"

They had expected the train to take them in to Victoria Station; instead it had delivered them to King's Cross. Cora looked at the station sign as the train slid to a halt and felt her nerves give a little premonitory twinge.

But André was already on his feet and making his way to the door. She followed him, close on his heels. She mustn't lose him now. If she lost him, she would be lost.

Now the terrors were back in force. If they engulfed her again, what would happen? Would she find when the darkness lifted that she was once more wandering in unknown territory, without a place to stay, without a name? Would she lose even this precarious identity as Cora Trent?

"André!" She caught his arm and clung to it in panic. "Don't . . . don't let's get separated!"

"Ah!" He patted her hand, pleased. "You take such good care of me."

They surged up the stairs with the crowd. Did André notice that he was half-carrying her? The closer they got to street level, the more she hung back. She would like to turn around and run to the opposite platform and take the next train back to Brighton without ever having set foot outside the station.

But she could never explain this to André. He thought she was just a simple and uncomplicated English girl. Perhaps she was. Who knew? She certainly didn't.

"London!" André threw his arms wide, or as wide as he could with Cora still hanging on like grim death. "We are in London!"

"It's filthy!" Cora said prissily. Black plastic sacks full of rubbish were heaped against the building. Orange peel, tattered old newspapers, cigarette butts, beer cans—you name it—littered the street. She looked around in growing dismay. Not even the Victorian Gothic extravaganza of St. Pancras Station in the distance lightened her mood, although it had never failed to amuse her before.

How had she known that?

"This is not, I think, the best part of town," André agreed. "If we begin walking, we must find better."

"That wouldn't be hard." Cora tried to pretend that her voice was not quavering.

But André didn't notice that, either, He had spotted St. Pancras Station and was walking towards it, pulling Cora along in his wake.

"*Fantastique!*" he said. "What is it?"

"You may not believe this—" she tried to shake off the mood, to pretend that this was just the pleasant day's outing they had intended—"but that's a railway station. St.

Pancras. The building on top started out as a hotel and I think they're trying to turn it back into one again." She no longer wondered how she knew all that.

"I stay there if they do! I send postcards to all my friends with the X for my room." Chortling happily, he strode along. *He* was having a great time.

She was regretting this escapade more every moment, every step. Was it too late to turn back? She halted, pulling André to a stop.

"What is wrong?" He looked down at her, puzzled.

"I—I don't feel well." It was true. She couldn't pretend any longer. The black shadows were fluttering just beyond her range of vision again, ready to swoop.

"You are train sick? But we are off the train now."

"I—I want to go back." Did she? The thought of the return journey made her feel even more ill. But so did the thought of staying. She felt herself swaying.

"Yes, yes, we see. First we get something to eat, yes?" He looked around hopefully. "Maybe if we walk up this way we find a nice place."

They turned their backs on the station and Cora felt herself swept along by his firm arm around her waist. Her vision had blurred, become almost double vision, as though she were seeing two scenes at once, neither of them clearly.

She closed her eyes, still being impelled along relentlessly. She had no idea where André was taking her, neither did he. All she had to do was remain conscious, not surrender to the shadows. It was better with her eyes closed, she didn't feel so queasy.

"Don't swoon, Cora," André said. "Keep walking. Don't swoon."

"Faint," she said. "I'm trying not to faint."

"Faint—swoon, don't do it!" He was moving faster now. "There are places ahead. We are nearly there. You can sit down. I will get you coffee, brandy for the stomach, and food. See, here are many restaurants. Which do you like: Indian, Italian, Greek— ?"

"I don't care," she whispered. "I don't want any food." But coffee was something else, that might help to disperse the shadows.

"Please, don't faint. We go in that one down the street. Those people coming out look happy. They have had a good meal. We will, too."

He hadn't warned her about the curb and she stumbled. Her eyelids flew open as she fought for balance.

"We have the light. Hurry!" André propelled her across the street and towards a restaurant where several people were emerging.

Where *she* was emerging!

Cora caught her breath, watching herself walk towards her. Her double-vision had split and achieved a life of its own and now her own doppelganger was bearing down on her. The doppelganger hadn't seen her yet; she was talking to the short burly man walking beside her. Cora didn't know him, but the others were familiar. She couldn't put names to them but—

"Cora, don't faint. We are almost there." Cora had stopped short and André was trying to encourage her on. Couldn't he see that there were two of her now? There was the Cora who was standing here clutching his arm tightly enough to cut off circulation—and there was the other Cora walking towards them who was going to look up at any moment and see her.

What happened when you were face to face with your

own doppelganger? When your eyes met, which one of you died?

"Cora, shall I carry you?" André started to pick her up and she shook him off.

"Don't you see me, André?" She had to know if she was the only one who could see her. "The other me—coming towards us. She's even wearing my clothes."

"Cora—?" André followed her gaze. "No one is wearing your clothes, Cora."

"Yes, she is!" That lovely maroon outfit—her Easter suit. Cora suddenly remembered the day she bought it. Giles was—Giles was right behind her! The other her! Giles was closing in on her!

"Look out!" she shrieked. "Run!"

They looked up and saw her. Her doppelganger began running towards her. So did Giles.

"No!" she screamed. "No!"

"Cora, what's the matter?" André stepped in front of her, trying to shield her from them. "Cora, what is it? Cora—?"

Connie went on screaming.

CHAPTER 31

Alison almost made it.

She was with Connie almost as far as the door. Then, suddenly, she was stretched out face down on the floor with the blood welling out of the wound in her neck.

There was blood everywhere. And noise.

Connie was deafened by the noise. It never sounded like that in the movies, not even when they put the sound up. It was manageable then, bearable, it wasn't these eardrum blasting explosions that took away your breath, your hearing. They talked about pop music making you deaf—they never told you about guns.

Henry grabbed her by the wrist as she stood looking down at Alison. He hurled the black coat around her shoulders. Probably he was shouting at her. She could see his mouth opening and shutting, but she couldn't hear a thing. Nothing except the overriding explosions in the background.

Maggie and Jaycee were back there, too. They had been the first to fall. They hadn't believed the gun Eddie was waving around as he accused Giles of cheating him over the takings was real. They had got in the way when Eddie had fired a warning burst, giving Giles the chance to snatch the gun from Eddie. But the gun had kept on firing and it seemed as though Giles couldn't turn it off.

Or perhaps Giles just didn't want to. He turned the gun on Eddie. And then on the others. By that time they had seen the look in his eyes and scattered, knowing that he was out of control.

She saw the next burst hit Angie and Jim, sending their bodies flying across the room, scattering blood. There was blood everywhere.

Blood and money.

This was the deserted house Eddie and Giles had been using as headquarters while they made the plans for the party that was to take place just a few miles away. After the party was under way, they had come back here with their friends to share out the proceeds.

Then the trouble had started as Eddie had accused Giles of holding out on him, of keeping most of the money he had collected from the ticket sales to his university friends for himself. It might even be true.

Giles had hotly denied it and the argument had got worse and worse, with some of the others joining in. Voices had grown louder, accusations more bitter. Until, suddenly, Eddie had produced the gun and the world had exploded around them.

Henry tugged at her wrist, pulling her off balance and dragging her towards the door. She knew what he must be saying, even though she couldn't hear a word. She was saying it to herself: *Run! Get out of here! You can't help the others! You can't! Get out! Save yourself! Run!*

Run! Her mind accepted it and recoiled from it at the same time. She couldn't leave Alison lying there . . .

Run! But she was already outside. Henry had slammed the door behind them, buying a few seconds' delay before the pursuit began. If Giles intended to pursue them. But he would, he had to. He'd gone mad—and they were the only witnesses.

Run! Henry was mouthing something at her. Dimly, she understood that she must put her arms into the sleeves of the coat and button it round her. Not for warmth, but to hide the pastel pink outfit she was wearing, pale colors that would make her stand out as a target.

Henry let go of her wrist as she struggled into the coat and buttoned it. Then, abruptly, Henry was gone. They had both been running as hard as they could, even while she fought her way into the coat. He must have turned down one of the side streets, thinking she was still with him.

But she wasn't. She was alone in the chill dank mist eddying out from the river. And the dark shadows were reaching out for her.

Run!

CHAPTER 32

"Mom!" Connie sobbed. "Mom!" The warm comforting arms closed around her.

"Connie!" They were both crying. "Oh, Connie, where have you been?"

"I don't know—" Connie raised her head and saw the baleful eyes staring at her. The terror swept over her again. "Don't let him near me!" she screamed. "Keep him away!"

"Don't worry, lass." The heavyset man had Giles in an iron grip. "He's not getting near you."

"This is ridiculous!" Giles stormed. "Let go of me at once!"

"We'll see about that," Thatchpole said. "There are a few things I want to know first. Where's Alison?"

"I don't know—" Giles was turning a delicate shade of green.

"She's dead," Connie sobbed. "He killed her! He killed them all!"

"Stan—no!" Dee screamed as Thatchpole transferred his grip to Giles's throat.

"Wait! Be calm—" André moved to help Dee pry Thatchpole's fingers from Giles's throat.

"Holy shit!" Heidi took André's place beside Connie.

"Were you kidding?" She looked at Connie's face. "You mean they're all dead? They really are?"

Connie nodded, forcing herself to remain still. She wanted to run, to hide, to slip back into the shadows and be carried away again. But she couldn't. She knew who she was now—and what had happened to her, to Alison, to the others.

And she knew that there was one last thing she could do for them. She had to go into court and testify against Giles. She had to see that he paid the price for what he had done.

In the distance, two figures in blue were hurrying towards the scene of the fracas. A crowd was gathering to watch. Giles had stopped struggling and was gathering his forces for one final effort.

"Make these people release me!" he demanded as the police arrived. "Do you know who I am? I'm Dean Abbott's son!"

"And no wonder the Dean took one look at you and had another stroke," Thatchpole said. "A son to be proud of! Arrest him!" he ordered the constables. "He's a dirty killer!"

"I think," one of the constables said, "we'll just all go along to the station and sort this out."

"I wondered," Dee said later, back at the hotel, "when I realized that the Dean's first stroke coincided with Connie's disappearance. But it seemed too far-fetched to imagine that he could have had anything to do with it."

"Young Giles more or less confessed to him. I gather the Dean caught him trying to wash away some bloodstains." Dr. Carson looked gloomily into the depths of his untouched drink. "But this was one scrape Daddy couldn't get him out of. The Dean recognized the enormity of it better than Giles did. He collapsed while Giles was halfway through trying to justify himself."

There was nothing wrong with Dr. Carson. Dee knew that now. Giles had simply been sowing seeds of mistrust on principle: divide and conquer. If she didn't trust anyone too completely, her chances of getting at the truth would be lessened. Meanwhile, Giles would move in on her, as he had been doing, and become the one she leaned on.

In extremis, however, it was Dr. Carson Giles had called to for help. Carson had gone over to the jail where Giles was being held and talked with him. Later, there had been another trip—after the police had notified the family—to bring Giles some basic necessities. Carson had had to try to comfort the tearful Mrs. Abbott and her daughters when he collected the things. It had not been a good day for Dr. Carson.

It had been a worse day for Stan Thatchpole. Dee topped up his drink. He had been drinking steadily since they got back to her room, but it didn't seem to have affected him at all. It would be better if it had.

"Giles won't get away with it, will he?" Heidi asked the question Connie hadn't wanted to voice. "When some expensive lawyer gets to work on the jury about this poor fatherless boy, terrible accident, diminished responsibility—and all that shit?"

"I think not," Carson said. "He ruined that chance when he killed Henry Daniels. That was premeditated and cold-blooded self-interest. The jury won't like it."

"Giles kept his sports car in the garage," Tanya said. She was still shocked and disbelieving. "That was how he met Eddie and learned about the empty flat. He told

Jaycee and—" She broke off and bent over Barney. She was going to have to rearrange her life and hopes. Maggie wasn't going back to the States and leave the field clear for her. Jaycee wasn't coming back to her, ever.

"There's a lot more to be learned," Carson said grimly, "but there's good reason to suspect that Giles had something going with the garage people long before the Acid House Party. He was in a position to know which students had bought new bikes and where they left them at night. No wonder there was such a spate of thefts around the campus." His mouth twisted. "No wonder Giles had such an expensive watch and wore designer clothes. That won't go down well with a jury, either."

"It won't, and that's a fact," Thatchpole said with grim satisfaction.

"Someday I trust you will explain this to me more fully." André was still beside Connie, holding her hand. "I would really like to understand it. Also, am I to understand that you are not returning to Brighton tonight?"

"Maybe tomorrow," Connie said, "with my mother. To collect my books . . . and things." The bloodstained notes hidden in the painting would be needed for evidence. Probably someone from the police would want to come along, too.

"Then you have to get back to your studies," Carson warned. "You have a lot of catching up to do."

"I'll do it," Connie said.

"It isn't far," André said. "I can come and see you often. If you don't mind—"

"I knew you could speak English better than you pretended," Connie said.

"A small deception." He shrugged. "Nothing compared to yours."

"Mine wasn't deliberate, I really *did* have amnesia." Connie shuddered. "I'm not sure I don't wish I still had it. Except for you, Mom—it's great to have you here, You're staying, aren't you?" Panic still lurked close to her.

"She needs you," Carson murmured unnecessarily. "And we'd rather like to keep you around ourselves."

The telephone rang. Dee moved to answer; it must be the police again. "Hello—?"

"Delia, where the hell have you been? I've been trying to get you all day! What the hell is going on over there?"

"I've been out," Dee said. "I've found Connie."

"I told you she was all right. When are you coming home?"

"She's not all right . . . not completely. I won't be back for a while. I'm staying here to take care of Connie."

"Wait a minute—you can't do that! What about me?"

"Here, dear—" Dee handed the receiver to Connie— "talk to your father." Dee found that she had nothing more to say to him. She was needed here and already Hal was receding into the mists of time. It might be better if Connie carried on with her schooling here; she'd have to testify at the trial and it would be too disruptive to go back and forth.

"Yes, Dad," Connie was saying, in a puzzled voice. "There are still three men in the room. Why do you . . . ? Mom—" she held out the receiver—"he wants to talk to you."

Dee walked away. It was time to top up Stan Thatchpole's drink again.

"Uh . . . she's kinda tied up right now, Dad," Connie said.

"Thanks," Thatchpole looked up at Dee with haunted eyes. "They want me to identify her, you know," he said.

"Tomorrow, or the next day. After they've got her looking— After they've tidied her up a bit, like."

"Oh, Stan!" Dee's heart wrenched. Alison, his baby, after lying dead for nearly a month. And it had so nearly been Connie, too. "Would you like me to go with you?"

"No, no. I wouldn't put anyone through that . . . But I'd like to think I could come back to you . . . afterwards. You're the only one who'll understand what—" He broke off and bowed his head.

"I'll be here," Dee said. "I'm going to be around for quite a while."